All of It, With You

Madeline Flagel

Copyright © 2023 Madeline Flagel

All rights reserved. No part of this publication may be reproduced, distributed, or transmitted in any form by any means, including photocopying, recording, or other electronic methods without the prior written permission of the author, except in brief quotations embodied in reviews and certain other noncommercial uses permitted by copyright law. For permission requests, please contact the author at the email address below.

Madeline Flagel

madelineflagelauthor@gmail.com

ISBN: 979-8-9878295-4-7 (paperback edition)

ISBN: 979-8-9878295-3-0 (ebook edition)

Cover Design by Rachel McEwan, Rachel McEwan Designs

Editing by Paige Lawson

Published May 2023

Published by Madeline Flagel

This is a work of fiction. Unless otherwise indicated, all the names, characters, businesses, places, events and incidents in this book are either the product of the author's imagination or used in a fictitious manner. Any resemblance to actual persons, living or dead, or actual events is purely coincidental.

Content Warning: this book contains explicit sexual content

To the readers that have a brother...get with his best friend.
It's good for the plot.

Chapter 1

Emilia

The entire back wall of the apartment is lined with windows, making Chicago easily visible from mine and Ford's bedrooms. It's so beautiful that I can almost forget he gets the bigger room out of the two. The deal was our parents would pay for our rent as long as we lived together, and since he's the only one attending school here, they get to dictate who's room is who's. I'm not even mad though, just happy to be away from them and in a brand-new city.

"Did you get all your luggage from the car?" Ford asks from behind me as I stare out the windows in the living room, mostly looking at my hazy reflection in the glass.

"I have to get one more. Unless you want to do that for me?" I reply with a cheeky smile.

He scoffs as he walks into his bedroom.

I'll take that as a no.

I turn around, walk past the kitchen, into the foyer, and out of the door. Making my way downstairs and out of the lobby to grab the last bit of luggage my brother wouldn't help me with. Thankfully, the luxury complex we're in has a private parking garage. Well, for an extra four hundred dollars a month, it does. I would never be able to afford this place on my own, so if living with Ford for a year is what it takes to have nice digs, then I can manage.

"We made it," I say to my mother on the other end of the phone as I pull my luggage back into the building.

"Wonderful. When do you start at Thirty8?" She asks dryly.

"Tomorrow. They said I can write a trial piece on whatever I want to see where I would best fit with the magazine."

"Emilia, that's great. Well, call your father and me often. We love you both. Tell Ford hello."

"Will do. Bye, mom." I say with little enthusiasm as I hang up. I'm already sweating from hauling this fucking suitcase. I'm not trying to listen to Colette's shrill voice in the process.

I return to our apartment and walk in, dragging my fifty-pound luggage behind me.

"Mom said hi," I say to Ford as he stands in the kitchen.

He nods and stretches his lips thin in a pressed smile. At least we both feel the same way about our parents. It's hard to form a relationship with people you hardly know. Our nanny was more of a mother than Colette.

"What should we do for our first night here?" I ask him as I sit on a barstool in front of the kitchen island.

"Well, we need food," Ford says as he peers into the stainless steel refrigerator. "But honestly, after traveling all day, the only thing I really want to do is get fucked up."

"Let's go out!" I squeal with excitement.

"Unpack first, groceries second, bad decisions last." He says as he claps his hands as if for us to start.

I nod and head to my room across from his. The apartment came fully furnished, so my bedroom is already decorated. Not typically how I would decorate it, but it'll do. The deep royal blue velvet on the headboard is the only color here. The rest is different tones of gray.

I throw my biggest suitcase on my bed first, rifling through it to find all my underwear and bras, then throwing those in a dresser drawer. I grab hangers for all my nice shirts, dresses, and jumpsuits to put in my walk-in closet. The shitty thing about Ford having the bigger room means his closet is twice the size of mine. Sure, I can walk into mine, but I can only take about three steps. *His* closet, on the other hand, you can at least walk five or six steps. He doesn't even need the closet space. The man wears four shirts on rotation.

"Emilia, hurry the hell up!" I hear him shout from outside my door. Not surprised he's already done unpacking with what little he has.

I keep my mouth shut — I'm not trying to start an argument, for his sake. As soon as I finish unpacking, I walk out to the living room and see Ford sitting on the couch, waiting for me, I presume.

"Let's go," I say, huffing loudly.

He shuts the TV off and lifts up, grabbing the keys to the apartment from the island before we're out the door. I follow him down the hall and into the elevators as we decide which grocery store to go to.

"What should we get?" He asks as the elevator doors open to the lobby.

"We need basics. Condiments, seasonings, let's get some fruit too and maybe some frozen shit since your cooking is ass." I laugh. He doesn't find it too funny though.

"I don't need to know how to cook anyways. Hopefully, I can find myself a nice, hot wife to do it for me." He smirks.

"You're annoying." I roll my eyes.

"Speaking of which," he says. "We haven't lived alone together before, so this might come as a shock, but if you think for one second I'm not going to be bringing girls back to the apartment, then you're dead wrong."

"Okay, so don't be a bitch when I bring guys back." I retort.

"Ew." He scoffs. *He's such a baby.* "Aren't you too young for that still?" He jokes.

"Ford." I say with tight lips. I'm three years younger than him, but he always acts like I'm a damn kid. On my birthday a couple of months ago, he made it a big deal that I was drinking too much. It was my *twenty-first* birthday.

We arrive at the market closest to our apartment and push through the door. I tell him I'll grab the fruit. He's on frozen food duty. I grab my favorites, strawberries and bananas first, then work my way to the others that sound good. Once I'm finished with those, I move on to the spice aisle.

"What did you get?" I ask Ford as he walks towards the cart with his hands full.

"Pizza, mostly." He says as he throws it in, toppling over the fruit. "What else do we need?"

"Go get some toilet paper and paper towels. I'll get the condiments. Then I think we're good," I reply before pushing the cart toward the aisle I need.

After I find everything on my mental list, *and then some*, I head to the aisle Ford's supposed to be in, only to find him chatting up a redhead in the aisle over. We haven't even been in this city for five hours, and already he's on the hunt. I don't know what girls see in him anyways. It must be his height. Girls love men over six-feet. Everything else sucks about him, though. He's annoying, doesn't pick up after himself, doesn't cook, isn't funny, I mean, the list can go on.

As I slowly push my cart to them, the redhead stops to look at me with confusion.

"You ready?" I ask him. He takes a breath and slightly rolls his eyes at me. I don't know what he wants me to do. I won't wait in another aisle while he tries to get her number. I'm hungry and ready to drink, and he's screwing up my plans.

"Give me a sec." He says quietly to me before turning to the woman. "So, Underground is the place to go, huh?" He asks her before she looks at him in disgust and walks away. "What the fuck, Emilia?" He lashes.

"I didn't do anything!" I laugh.

"She probably thought you were my girlfriend or something. Why couldn't you just wait until I was done?"

"I don't know why she would think that, Ford. Is she stupid? We look the exact same." I snap back at him while we move to checkout.

"Ew, no, we do not, don't ever say shit like that again." He chuckles, still with a displeased look on his face.

Ford and I do look *similar*, but I know how pissed he gets when I tell him we look identical. His hair is black, darker than mine. But our eye color is the same, brown flecks on top of hazel, just like our mothers. The only thing Colette ever did for us was give us pretty eyes.

We pay for our groceries and head back to the apartment to get ready for a night out in our new city. The redhead at the market talked him into some club near us, so that's where we're going.

"You're wearing that?" I question Ford as I shut my bedroom door and face him in the kitchen.

"Me? You look like you're going to a fucking funeral." He snaps back.

"I can only hope my friends dress like this at my funeral." I smugly say. I hardly feel black leather pants and a strapless top is funeral attire, but I don't think Ford's actually attended one before, so I'll let it slide. "Let's hit the road!

I need a drink." I say as I throw my hand up. He follows behind and locks the door.

"We're taking an Uber, right?" I ask him as we get into the elevator.

"It's like, an eight-minute walk, Em. You'll be fine."

"I'm in heels." I whine.

"Suck it up, buttercup." He says as the elevator doors open.

We walk outside, and the bitter chill of the night washes over me, sending a wave of goosebumps down my bare arms. Maybe going strapless was not the right move for tonight.

"This way," Ford says as he waves his hand, taking the lead with GPS on his phone. I follow him, clutching myself as I wrap my arms around my body to keep warm.

"IDs." The bouncer says as we make our way in line. I take mine from my small crocodile purse and hand it to him. He looks it over, then hands it back after checking Ford's first.

"Have a good night." The bodyguard says as we move past him inside. The club is booming, completely jam-packed while colored lights sweep over everyone in the same rhythm as the roaring music.

"Over there!" I yell as I point to the bar. I push through the crowd as Ford follows. "Old Fashioned, please." I smile at the bartender. "Can you put a little extra sweetener in there too?" I lean over on the bar a little more, pushing my breasts together, using every advantage of these D cups I can. He smiles and nods as he grabs a glass and starts on my drink.

"I'll take one too, and you can hold the extra sweetener in mine. I'm not a pussy." Ford laughs with the bartender.

I roll my eyes with a cheeky smile at both of them. Ford nods in a direction behind me, and I turn to look as the bartender hands me my drink, two open seats near a smaller bar in the back corner. *Perfect.* The bartender hands Ford his drink, and we push through the crowd further. The sea of people swarming in the middle is insane, like sardines packed in a can. I move to the right and instantly get bumped in the shoulder by a man, spilling the entirety of the drink on myself. I look up at him, the urge to yell already caught in my throat, but I stop when I see him. Dark wavy hair and light eyes. *Oh my God.* This man is hot. A warm smile rests on my face as soon as my eyes catch his.

"I'm so sorry!" He yells to me over the DJ booth right next to us. "Let me get you another!"

I bite my bottom lip and nod, still in a smile before I look to find Ford in front of me, but the sea of sardines already split us up. Mystery man extends his hand to me as he starts pushing through the crowd to the bar in the back. I grab him as he leads us, only for a short time.

"I am so sorry. It's rough in there." He laughs, his voice softer since we're further from the music. "I'm Jacob." He says, extending his hand for me to shake.

"Emilia." I smile.

"So what are you drinking, Emilia?"

"Old Fashioned, please." I keep my grin, not daring to tell him I want it sweeter.

He holds his smile as he nods, asking the bartender for my drink.

"Thank you," I say.

"Are you from Chicago?"

"Just moved here today," I reply. "You?"

"Moved here about six years ago."

"What did you move here for?"

"A girl." He raises his eyebrows. "You?"

"A job." I say with pursed lips. "Where's that girl now?"

"She left me as soon as I got here," he laughs. "Ah, shit," he says as his sight moves past me and he grabs onto my shoulders, turning me around. "See that guy throwing up in the trash can over there?" He points. My head nods slightly while I hone in on my vision. "That's my buddy, I should probably get him home." He turns to face me, his grip still on my shoulders before his hand falls down my arm with the slightest touch, and his fingertips graze mine. "I hope to see you again, Emilia."

"Maybe you will." I grin as he walks backward slowly, waiting until his arm reach is too far and our fingertips can't touch any longer before he turns around and walks to his friend.

I sip my drink and involuntarily wrinkle my nose, coughing slightly. It's more bitter than I'm used to. My eyes wander around the club, bobbing my head slightly to the music as I take it all in.

My new city.

I glance over to the table Ford said we should sit at, and I see him, along with a blonde bimbo in a bright pink dress. Ford is sitting on the stool while she's in between his legs, her lips plastered on his. I would rather *die* than see this visual. I walk up to the table, and Ford sees me out of the corner of his eye, unlocking his lips from the woman.

"You ready to go?" He asks me as the blonde stares right at him with a smile.

"I guess." I say as I shrug my shoulders. We haven't been here long at all, in fact, I think the walk over took longer, but I'm so jet-lagged. Laying in bed sounds a lot better than being here right now. He takes the blonde in hand while I finish what was left of my drink, and we shuffle through the crowd and out the door to walk back to our place.

Just Ford, Pinky, and I.

Chapter 2

Emilia

I'm so hungry and can't remember if I ate anything today, either. Thank god we got some kind of groceries earlier.

"It was nice meeting you." The blonde says as she closes Ford's bedroom door.

I give her a half-ass smile before going into my room and throwing on gray sweats and a sports bra. I head back to the kitchen and pre-heat the oven, taking a frozen supreme pizza out of the freezer. I walk around the island into the living room and sit on the gray sectional. Turning the TV on until the oven is ready. I hear pinky giggling, and I silently pray to whoever will listen that these walls between us are thick. The oven beeps, and I rise up, moving back to the kitchen to put my pizza in.

Then I hear it — the first moan.

Fuck.

I set the timer on the microwave and walk back to the living room, turning the TV up a little louder. Thankfully, *The Real Housewives* arguing at a wine tasting drown out the sound. Once the microwave beeps, I walk back to take the pizza out and put a slice on my plate. Ford's door swings open and he walks out in just his sweatpants. I flash him a repulsive expression as he smiles, grabbing a plate from the cupboard and getting himself three slices.

"Be nice." He says. "That could be your sister-in-law in there."

I roll my eyes and sigh. Bringing the pizza back to my comfy spot on the couch. I hear Ford's door close and I have peace and quiet for at least fifteen minutes, besides the housewives still yelling at each other. As I'm going to get a second piece of pizza, a loud thumping comes from Ford's room. Over and over again. I groan in agony as I throw the pizza on my plate and shut the TV off before walking into my bedroom and slamming the door. I don't know how we will make it through an entire year living together. This is *night fucking one*. I finish my food and shut off my light, crawling into bed under my covers. The bedspread they provided is really nice, fluffy too. The sheets feel like silk, which I'm all for. I try to drift to sleep, but the looming thought of my first day at work tomorrow is racing through my mind. I know I'm qualified enough for this job, but this is a full-on magazine, a magazine *I will write for*. It's my dream job, and I landed it. I should be proud of myself. I have nothing to be nervous about, except that I still have no idea what I'm going to write my freestyle article on.

Thirty8 is based on fashion, dating, health, and beauty. I would love to write about real-world issues like, *Should Education Be Free*, or maybe The *Dangers Of Plastic And Pollution*, but that's not what this magazine is about...I'll probably have to stick with something like *Five Ways To Have The Best Orgasm* or *Best Winter Cocktails For Your Holiday Party*.

My eyes flutter shut as my mind grows silent, allowing me to drift to sleep peacefully.

Seven-thirty in the morning, my alarm blasts through my room. I walk to my bathroom sluggishly, flicking on the light. I toggle with the shower handle to figure out which way is hot and cold. The shower is sleek, with dark tile and a long bench running down the length of the back wall. Easily could fit three people in here, not that I have any plans to do that, though. Once my water is scolding hot, *the perfect temperature if you ask me*, I undress and get in. I've got at least an hour and a half to get ready and be at my new job, so I'm doing well on time. Once I'm finished, I get out and dry off before wrapping the towel around my body so I can dry my hair. I blow dry it straight with my round brush, only so the ends of my hair will curl inwards. The peak of my hair falls just above my waistline when I wear it straight like this, and right after it's blowdried, it looks more like shiny chocolate than a dull brown, which I prefer. After my hair is finished, I work my way to my closet and pull out a baby blue suit set with a cropped blazer. I've had this outfit planned ever since they told me I got the job. I grab a white tank for underneath that ends right where the jacket does and grab my little white purse to go along with it. After throwing all the pieces on the bed, I walk back to my bathroom and start on my makeup, keeping it simple and fresh. I use brown shades over and under my eyes to make the green from my iris pop. After I change, I head straight to the refrigerator to make myself a fruit bowl.

"Sleep well?" I snark to Ford as he exits his room. He grins slightly as he rubs his eye with the back of his hand. I peer through his door, noticing pinky is nowhere to be found. "Where did she go?"

"I called her an Uber last night." He says flatly before he yawns and throws a pod into the Keurig.

"Make me one, please," I say to him over my shoulder. "So, no sister-in-law for me then, huh?" I ask sarcastically.

He chuckles before removing his cup and placing a new one in the holder for my coffee.

"What time will you be off work?" He asks as he yawns again.

"Four or five, probably," I say before I take my first bite from my bowl.

"Cool. What are you cooking for dinner?"

"Yeah, fuck right off. You can order delivery for us. It's my first day, Ford." I whine.

"I know, I know. I'm kidding. Relax, Em." He says softly. "Good luck. I'm going back to bed." He says as he hands me my coffee and walks back to his room.

I finish my breakfast, grab my keys, and head out.

I don't know what I expected the building to look like, but this wasn't it. All encased with glass, at least thirty stories high. Walking in are two large glass escalators and what seems to be an entire food court on the second level. People bustle in and out of the large lobby and my stomach knots.

With no idea where I'm supposed to be going, a new city, a new job, my nerves are struck.

I'm way out of my comfort zone.

I look around and adjust myself, getting my bearings until I see a large desk with three people behind it.

"Hi, My name is Emilia Bardot. I'm here to see Kathy Reign," I say to the bright-eyed receptionist.

"Hello! Yes, we've been expecting you." She says excitedly with a large smile. "You can take the elevators around the corner to the sixth floor. That will be your department." She says as she motions in the direction I'm supposed to be heading.

I thank her and walk that way. Rounding the corner, I see four elevators along a wall.

"Six," I say to the gentleman near the buttons. He presses it for me as the elevator doors close. We move up in floors, one by one, until landing on mine. As the doors slide open, I immediately see people holding papers, walking back and forth, and looking in a hurry. I walk out as the doors close behind me, trying to find someone who looks somewhat authoritative.

"Emilia?" A voice calls for me from behind. I turn around to see a lengthy woman, very thin, with big blonde curls draping past her shoulders.

"Hi." I smile

"I'm Kathy. I'm so glad you're here! Let me show you around quickly, and I'll bring you to your desk." She says with a smile so big her cheek fillers nearly hit her eyes. I follow her around as she points and speaks.

"This is where the printer and fax is. Over here is what we call the bullpen. Your desk is in there." She says as she points to the middle of the room, full of cubicles. "Here are some editor offices, and my office is right here." She says as she points to the opposite side with private offices and their glass doors. "Food is on the second floor, you get an hour and a half for lunch, and everything is free there. Just use your key card." She says as we make our way inside the cubicles in the center of the room.

"Key card?" I ask.

"Yes, we've got to get a photo of you for your card. I'll have it printed by noon." She says as we arrive at an empty cube. "Here is your home!" She excitedly says.

The cubicles are a blueish gray, each with the same style of black chairs. Mine is bleak compared to the person next to me — decorated to the max, with bright colors and a mass of photos pinned to the walls. It makes mine look even worse.

"Let me get your photo really quick, then you can get settled. Did Riley brief you on what to do today? The freestyle edit?" Kathy says to me as we move out of the center, near a plain white wall.

"Yes, she did." I smile.

"Great, just need that by the end of the day today, and we will get you placed tomorrow." She says as she waves for me to pin my back against the wall. She holds up her phone, and I smile with closed lips. My lips are naturally full, but when I smile, it seems my top lip becomes flatter, so I try to smile with my mouth closed in photos all of the time. "Beautiful. Okay, I'll have this back to you in a bit." She says with a soft smile as she moves past me.

I pull out the chair at my desk and sit before turning on the iMac, and I peek over my cube to my neighbor to get some decorating ideas when she catches my glance.

"Hi! I'm Katie." She says as she slides her chair out from her desk.

"Emilia," I say as I reach out to her. She takes my hand in hers and shakes it gently. She's pretty, a little plain. No makeup, dark-rimmed glasses, cute bangs though.

"You're the new columnist, right?" She asks.

"That is correct." I smile.

"Awesome! Have you lived here long?"

"Just moved here yesterday."

"Oh my gosh, really? How exciting." She says with a wide grin. "Do you live close?"

"At the Saranac." I reply.

"Close to me! I'm at Maplewood." She says.

I saw those apartments, not as luxurious as mine, but she also probably doesn't have her parents paying for everything like we do. I guess that's *one* perk of your family owning a large media company. We chat some more as I scoot my chair closer to my computer. I really need to get started on this article, and I still have no idea what the fuck I'm going to write. As our chatter slows, I get to work. I decided on *Fifteen Places To Have Great Sex Besides The Bedroom*. It's daring and perfect for the magazine. If I can write this well, I could be placed more on the health side, which could open more possibilities for me writing things I care about.

As lunchtime rolls around, Katie invites me to check out the food court with her. We get into the elevator and go down to the second floor. The doors open and there is quite possibly every food you could imagine, from smoothies and pressed juice to fried chicken. And all of this for free? We each pick our own food and meet at a table in the center.

"How long have you worked here?" I ask her as I twist open my diet coke.

"Four years. I love it." She smiles.

"Are you a columnist as well?" I ask.

"I work on graphics for the articles." She replies as she opens her salad.

We talk for the entire hour of lunch about anything and everything. I'm interested in her life, as it vastly differs from mine — besides, I don't have many friends. I've never actually had a certain place to call home, so it's not like I even had a fighting chance to make them anyways. The amount of times we moved from city to city is unreal. Being in Chicago for a year will be the longest I've lived anywhere in my entire life. So I'm happy to get to know Katie.

Once we're back at our desks, I buckle down and finish the article, with thirty minutes until four o'clock. *Perfect timing.* I find Kathy again to turn it in and hope for the best. She tells me I'm free to leave, so I do just that. Exchanging numbers with my new friend Katie before I head home.

I can't believe this is my life, my dream job, not my dream office...just yet, but still, nonetheless, I'm happy and content and ready for whatever this year in Chicago brings for me.

Chapter 3

Emilia

"Emilia!" The boys shout as I enter my apartment.

"What the fuck are you doing here?" I ask Rhett, who's sitting on the couch next to Ford.

"Hello to you too, Em." Rhett says.

I'm not sure if it's the look of confusion or disappointment on my face that prompts my brother to tell me why his childhood best friend is in our new place...*in Chicago*.

"Rhett is moving to the city. I told him he could stay with us until he finds a place. Don't tell mom."

Ford was lucky growing up. Rhett's parents worked with ours, so anywhere we would move — Rhett would too. *Unlucky* for me, it was like I had *two* idiot brothers.

"And, um, where will he be sleeping?" I ask as I set my purse down and take my blazer off. Throwing them both on the island.

"My room, the couch in there is a pull-out." He replies. His answer digs into my soul: his room is big enough for a pull-out couch, while mine is only big enough for one chair. Very clear on who the fucking favorite child is. I press my lips thin and nod as I take the information in, hating that three adults will be sharing a two-bedroom apartment for god knows how long.

"Well, I'm going to get comfy clothes on. You boys can figure out dinner," I say as I walk to my bedroom and shut the door. I haven't seen Rhett since the beginning of the year, but he still looks the same, with just a few more tattoos. When he was younger, his hair was longer and more blonde. Now that it's shaved short, it almost looks brown. His entire arm is covered in tattoos. The last time I saw him, he only had a quarter sleeve. Other than that, he's still the same old, annoying, brainless brother I never wanted…Rhett Adler.

"So what's it going to be?" I ask them as I come out of my room while I roll my sweatpants up by the waist and sit on the chair in the living room.

"Chinese?" Rhett says as he scrolls through his phone.

"Fine, get me—"

"Sesame chicken, I know." Rhett cuts me off. I give him a half smirk as my eyes roll slightly to the back of my head.

I curl up my legs in the chair and pull my tank up from the low neckline.

"Don't get any ideas." Ford says to Rhett as he catches Rhett's eyes falling on my hands that are adjusting my top.

"Ew!" Rhett and I squeal.

"Get fucking real." I say to Ford.

"She wishes." Rhett laughs.

"Shouldn't you be married by now?" I jokingly ask Rhett.

"Me?" He says with wide eyes as he points to his chest.

"I just figured since you're like, almost thirty." I laugh again, only trying to piss him off. He's just a couple of months older than Ford, both of them only being three years older than me.

We sit and talk about my work and when Ford starts classes. Rhett lets us know he just got hired by a construction company here, and that's why he's making the move. It was always their dream to have Ford design the buildings and Rhett construct them. It's kind of sweet to see them in their adult years still following it. Ford decided the architecture program here in Chicago would be a better fit for him, and I guess it just kind of worked out that I got hired at a magazine hereafter.

Our food arrives, and Rhett grabs it from outside of the door.

"We're going to go out tonight. Wanna come?" Ford asks me as we start divvying up the food.

"I've got to be at work by nine tomorrow," I say as I find my sesame chicken and rice.

"Oh hell, that's plenty of time to sleep in." Rhett says to me.

"I don't know. I want to just relax tonight. Go without me this time." I say before I take a bite.

"It's your first night here, so we gotta get you laid." Ford says to Rhett.

"I still can't fucking believe you already pulled ass in this city." Rhett laughs.

"You guys are gross." I say with a mouthful of food.

"You're just jealous." Ford replies.

"Of what? Fucking a bimbo with fake tits? Yeah, I'll pass. Thank you." I scowl.

"She sounds awesome." Rhett chimes in.

Ford motions to the size of her breasts with his hands to Rhett... *completely exaggerating*.

We laugh together — well, my laugh is directed more toward how stupid these two are.

While the boys get ready to go out, I make myself comfortable on the linen sectional, wrapping my legs up in a white fuzzy blanket and settling in the perfect nook between two cushions.

"Don't wait up!" Ford calls from the foyer as they walk out.

Finally, peace and quiet.

I turn on Bravo and binge-watch Southern Charm until my eyes get heavy. Eventually, I glance at my phone and see it's already midnight — I went down a fucking rabbit hole with these people from Charleston tonight and didn't even realize the mindless hours that passed. I shut the TV and the living room lights off, leaving only one light on in the kitchen for the guys. I crawl into bed and not long after, hear the front door open, followed by the boys muffled voices and the faint sound of a woman. I groan into my pillow. I can't believe I'm going to go through another night of this. As I pull the pillow on top of my ear to muffle any sounds from tonight's extracurriculars, I faintly hear the creaking of my door handle turning, followed by the unlatching of my door from the frame. I swing the pillow off my head and see Rhett quietly working his way into my room, shutting the door behind him.

"What the fuck are you doing?" I ask. My voice strained between a yell and a whisper.

"I can't stay in Ford's room tonight." He says quietly, visibly intoxicated. "He wanted to let you know Pinky's back?" He says with a light laugh.

"Oh, Jesus, the bimbo." I say as I sit up.

Rhett sits on the end of my bed as I look at him. Only the city lights of Chicago shine through my room.

"The way he described her, I thought she would be a lot hotter. I mean, she's alright, just not my type." He says as he lays near the foot of my bed with his arms underneath his head.

"Rhett, you're type is anything with a pussy, don't kid yourself." I laugh, as does he.

"We're gonna check out the gym here tomorrow. Wanna come?" He asks as he turns his head to look at me.

"Yeah, can you guys wait until I'm home?"

"Sure." He says as he starts to close his eyes.

"Okay, fun times over. I gotta get my beauty sleep." I say as I lightly kick him on the side to make his eyes open.

"Fuck, you'd have to sleep for eighty years." He says as he lifts up with a smile. I grab a pillow next to me and throw it at him as he walks away.

What an ass.

Chapter 4

Emilia

Don't freak out, don't freak out Emilia. Holy. Fuck. I can not believe they are going to run my article in next month's issue. It was a freestyle. A fucking *trial* freestyle. And it's going to be printed.

Kathy found me straight away this afternoon to tell me the news. I'm in shock...or possibly on the verge of having a heart attack, but I've stood in this bathroom for over ten minutes trying to remain calm and lower my pulse.

I can't believe it.

Compose yourself Em. We're professionals, after all.

I run my hands down my stomach to flatten my long sleeve tucked into my waist snatching dress pants before I walk back to my cubical and sit, still staring at the emptiness around my desk. I hardly have any photos worth putting up here to begin with. None really with my parents, *not like I would hang those up anyway*, Ford would rather die than take a photo with me, no true friends I would remotely care enough to think about daily — Therefore, these gray walls of nothingness will remain bland for the foreseeable future.

"So...what did she say?" I hear Katie's soft-spoken voice from behind me.

"Oh my god, Katie. They're running the article for next month's issue!" I excitedly say in a loud whisper. I don't have anyone else to share the good news with, so telling someone feels good.

"Holy shit! Way to go!" She cheers with me in the same whisper tone. "Let's go out and celebrate tonight! My treat."

"I'm in." I say with a large smile. At least it's the weekend, no work the next two days, so I can get as fucked up as I feel like tonight.

The hours go by quickly as I read through and edit other columnists work. Kathy said she would like me to focus on the magazine's health section, *another win for me today*. In the meantime though, to get accustomed to Thirty8 and their style, I'm stuck editing and proofreading other articles written by my peers.

Katie said we could go back to The Underground. I agreed since I'm somewhat familiar, but let her know my brother and his friend will likely tag along.

"I'll text you in a bit," I say to Katie as I get up to leave my desk and make sure I wave to Kathy on my way out.

I walked to work today since the weather was in the seventies. Everyone at work was saying this would probably be the last nice day we will have for a while. I'm not familiar with Chicago weather but I know it snows. I won't be walking to work when that happens.

As I come to my building, I walk in and nod to the concierge before pressing the button for the elevators. I'm excited to tell Ford about my day, but I'm unsure if he will care.

"Guess what?" I say as soon as I step through the foyer.

Ford is reclining on the couch, and Rhett is sitting on a stool in the kitchen. Both of their eyes glued to their phones. "That article I wrote yesterday...they're going to publish it in next month's issue." I say with a grin so big my cheeks hurt.

"What!" Ford says excitedly as he jerks his body up.

"That's amazing!" Rhett says at the same time he sets his phone down.

Well, they made me feel much more excited about it than I already am.

"Do you guys want to go out and celebrate tonight?" I ask them with a smile. "Gym first?"

"Absolutely." Rhett says.

"Yes." Ford says at the same time.

I nod with assurance and head to my room to find something to work out in. I only started going to the gym because of these two, really. I mainly just do cardio, so I feel better about what terrible food choices I make. Those boys, though, take fitness very seriously. Ford isn't as bulky as Rhett is yet, but I know he's working up to it. I grab black Nike shorts and a matching sports bra to throw on. Tossing my hair up in a messy ponytail as I walk out my bedroom door.

"Ready?" I ask Rhett as he puts his cut-off t-shirt on in the kitchen. He makes it hard not to notice how each muscle in his stomach is defined — with what little body fat percentage he has on him.

Ford walks out of his bedroom wearing something similar, and we all leave the apartment together, going up the elevator eight more floors to the gym.

"I'll be over here." I say to the boys as I point to the stair master. They both head to the free weights, and I hop on, sticking air pods in my ears and scrolling through my playlist, eventually landing on some rap song Rhett introduced me to.

I climb, and climb, as the sweat beads on my skin and a pool of it settles in my cleavage. I consistently stay on this death trap of a device for forty minutes, which is a new record for me. *It's that brutal.*

"How ya doing?" Rhett asks as he walks to the side of my machine. I give him a thumbs up, the only thing I can do while my heavy breathing takes precedence over my voice.

"I forgot my water." I say with winded breaths.

Rhett hands me his, and I take a swig and hand it back. "Thanks." I say as my hands move to my hips to try to open my lungs. "When did you get this?" I move his cutoff over a little bit to expose his chest. His arm tattoo goes over his shoulder and pours lightly onto one of his pecks. As I point and poke him in the new tattoo, I feel him. Hard, like a brick. Just pure muscle with that man.

"Like three or four months ago." He says as he takes a drink of his water.

"Hm." I nod.

"What, you don't like it?" He asks as his nose wrinkles slightly and his head cocks to the side.

"No, I didn't say that. It's interesting, I guess." I say as my machine finally stops, and I get off.

Rhett raises his eyebrows in curiosity as he brings his water bottle to his lips.

It's not that I don't like it...I think I like it a little too much. The shading is nice, and the artwork is top-notch — it contours perfectly with the dips from his muscles.

"You guys ready? What time are we leaving for the club?" Ford asks as he reaches us.

"We can go back, eat, and get ready?" I question.

"Yep." Rhett replies.

"Good for me." Ford says.

We walk past the locker rooms and out of the glass doors, grabbing the open elevator. My stomach rumbles, and I remember we don't have many ingredients that I could actually cook a meal with.

"Do you guys want takeout or want me to cook?" I ask the boys as we're in the elevator.

"Cook." They simultaneously say with wide grins.

My nanny, Elizabeth, taught me how to cook. It was one of my favorite things to do as a child. I didn't play with dolls, didn't play with friends... I was making crepes by the time I was eleven. I enjoy cooking now into my adult years. It just happens less and less with jobs and grown-up responsibilities. I can't just stand in the kitchen all day and whip shit up.

As we get off the elevator, I scroll through my phone and order the ingredients I need.

"Scallops with a vegetable risotto?" I ask them as we walk into our apartment.

They both agree, and I place confirmation on my delivery. *I knew they would agree.* The number of times we've had meals together, I know what both boys like and dislike. Rhett hates tomatoes and raisins. Ford doesn't like raw onions, but if they are cooked, he can manage. I've made this for them a time or two, and it's always a crowd favorite. Super easy too. I'm excited to finally settle down enough for a home-cooked meal.

I walk into my bedroom and immediately start stripping my clothes off, starting my shower to get this sticky sweat off. Once I'm finished, I wrap the white towel around my body and brush my hair. These towels are smaller and hardly fit over my chest, so I hold it in place as I walk to my closet next to see if anything jumps out at me for what to wear tonight. A knock comes from my door, and my neck snaps to look. I walk towards it and open it to see Rhett standing on the other side.

"Is my chain in here?" He asks as he barges in.

"Chain?" I question.

"Yeah, my gold chain." He says as he moves closer to my bed, plucking it from the top of my bedspread. It must have come off when he laid down here briefly last night. "Can you put it on?" He asks as he hands it to me. I grab it with one hand, as the other is holding the towel up around my breasts.

"Hold on, can you —" I say as I try to shift myself to have two hands free. I ultimately decide to press my body firmly on Rhett's back to keep the towel in place. Once I'm secured, I raise my hands and stand on the tips of my toes a bit to clasp his necklace around him. I grab my towel between us and back away.

"Thanks." He says as he slowly turns around, his eyes falling to the tops of my breasts peaking out of the towel.

"Goodbye." I say as I raise my eyebrows and nudge my head to the door. He smiles lightly and leaves, shutting my door behind him.

I continue to get ready until I hear Ford call outside my bedroom that the groceries are here. I quickly grab shorts and a t-shirt to throw on, so I can start dinner. My hair and makeup are done, at least, so I'm way ahead of schedule here anyways. I walk out to the kitchen and get started on the risotto, which takes ten more minutes than the scallops. I open the white wine next and pour a glass.

I love cooking with wine. Well, I love drinking the wine I'm supposed to be cooking with.

"Smells good," Rhett says as he comes out of the bedroom, holding a shirt. I give him a quick glance over my shoulder before I continue to stir. Working with both pans, searing the scallops in one and adding broth to the other until finished. I get three dishes out from the cupboard and start to plate our dinner, risotto on the bottom, topped with four scallops each. I look and admire my first plate that's completed. Elizabeth would be proud.

"Dinner's done!" I call to the boys as I set the plates on the island.

"Oh god, I can't wait." Ford says with excitement.

"Thanks, Em." Rhett says as he takes a seat on the stool.

I grab two glasses of water and slide them to the boys before I grab my wine glass and walk around the island, taking the last open seat.

"You even cut up lemons for the scallops?" Ford asks as he squeezes one over his plate. I turn my head to look at him and smile as I take my first bite. *Perfection.*

"Damn, this is fucking amazing." Rhett says with a mouthful.

I chuckle a bit. This is always my favorite part —people enjoying what I made.

We eat dinner, and I tell them that my new friend Katie will be joining us for the celebration tonight. They are equally excited that I made a friend, but then, of course, the questions I knew were coming pour in.

Is she hot?

How big are her tits?

Is she single?

I answer their questions to the best of my abilities, only confirming she is single.

"Okay, boys, I'm going to get changed." I say as I take the last bite and stand up from the stool to bring my dish to the sink.

I go back into my room and stand in my closet. I have no idea what the fuck to wear. *Black, brown, black, brown* — it seems those are the only colors I own.

I settle on a slinky silk brown top and jeans with a beautiful diamond detail on the side. I fumble with the top. The small strings in the back are hard for me to tie myself, especially with the crisscross detail it needs to be secured in. I hold the strings behind me as I walk out of my bedroom, trying to find the first person to help me tie this. My eyes land on Rhett in the kitchen, cleaning up the ingredients I cooked with.

"I can get that." I say to him as I walk closer.

"It's okay. You cooked, you shouldn't have to clean." He replies.

"Can you help me tie this really quick?" I ask as I walk to him and turn around. He puts down the spatulas and wipes his hands with a towel before grabbing the strings from me. His fingers lightly graze my back as he fiddles with them, and the sensation causes my arms to instantly break out in goosebumps.

"This tight?" He asks.

"A little tighter please." I say. I can't wear a bra with this top. The straps are too thin, so I need it as tight as possible to ensure these puppies stay locked in all night. "Perfect." I say to him. "Thank you."

"Mhm." He says as he turns to finish cleaning up.

I head back to my room and finalize the last-minute details of getting dressed before I wait in the kitchen and sip my wine as the boys finish getting ready themselves. Ford walks out first in black pants and a button-down shirt, Rhett follows with a white graphic t-shirt and nice jeans. The bright white of the shirt makes his skin tone look deeper than usual.

"You boys clean up nice." I say with a smile. I quickly text Katie to see if she's ready. She tells me she'll be there in twenty, perfect timing for us. I can't wait to get fucked up, and most importantly, I can't wait to celebrate *me* tonight.

Chapter 5

Emilia

I thought this place was packed when we came here last. Tonight, though — *Holy shit*. We'll be lucky to even get to the bar for a drink.

"Should we get a table?" Ford yells over the music.

"Bottle service?" I smile.

"Don't tell mom." He says as he holds our parent's credit card with a grin.

I nod my head yes as he leaves to find out how we can reserve one, I would assume these have to be booked well in advance, but Ford has a way of getting what he wants when money is involved. I suspect he tips excruciatingly well.

My eyes wander around the club, comparing the hectic atmosphere to the last time I was in this place. The same colored lights still flash and the music still blasts through the speakers, but the sea of people looks more like a mosh pit this time. My eyes shift back to the entrance and I finally spot Katie coming through. I wave to her, grabbing her attention almost instantly.

"Hi!" I shout to her as we hug. "Katie, this is Rhett." I say to her.

Her eyes light up as she sees him and extends her hand. They shake as Ford comes back with a host.

How does he do it?

"This way." The host says as we follow her through the crowd to a large booth on the side of the dance floor. We huddle in, and she tells us a server will be right over.

"Katie, this is Ford." I introduce them as we take a seat.

"Nice to meet you." She says to Ford as his face grows wide with a grin.

In the office, Katie is dressed down, her face hiding behind glasses. Tonight though, her dark hair is perfectly curled, and her makeup is glammed to perfection. I'm assuming she has contacts in because I can see that her natural eyelashes are long and full — something I haven't noticed before.

"You look great!" I say loudly over the music to her.

"Me?" She shouts. "You look fucking stunning." She says with a large smile.

I love her already.

"So which one is your brother?" She asks.

"Ford." I say as we look over at the guys in their conversation.

She smiles and nods. "So, you just live with both of them?"

"For the time being," I smirk.

"They are single-handedly the two hottest men I've ever seen." She giggles.

"Sick." I laugh with her and shove her arm slightly. I look at the boys and try to capture what she might see in them. Ford's hair is medium length, very dark, and he has light green eyes…I *guess* that could be appealing to other women. Rhett's hair is short, almost buzzed, and the stubble on his face highlights his sharp jaw. Both men take care of their bodies, but Rhett…his shape is fuller, and more defined. I could see where the attraction to Rhett could be. He gives off the vibe that he's easygoing — never worried or stressed. I admire him in that way, and he's always been very supportive of me. I could imagine if he ever nutted up and committed to someone, he would do the same for her.

"Vodka or Tequila?" Ford shouts as he glances over the table menu.

"Vodka," I reply. "It comes with juices, right?" I ask.

He nods and in an instant, our bottle girl arrives. Ford orders for us, and we sit and wait until our drinks come. The music is loud, and the colored lights turn to strobe's as the songs change. We all hold conversation over the music as the guys mainly ask Katie what she does at the magazine. I'm sure they are *both* eyeing her. For a slight second, I consider the possibility of her and Ford. I'm always nervous when he brings girls home, I don't want one of those sluts becoming my family, but Katie, I actually wouldn't mind. I quickly snap out of my thoughts as our bottle of Grey Goose arrives with tall decanters of cranberry, orange, and pineapple juice. Rhett distributes the drinks to us and issues a toast *for me*.

"Congratulations on your big day Em. You deserve it." He says as he raises his glass and stares into my eyes.

We all cheers and take our first sips.

"Let's dance!" Katie shouts as she grabs my hand and moves us out of the booth.

We stay close to our table but mix in with the crowd. The DJ is playing an EDM version of *Woman* by Doja Cat as Katie and I jump and sway with the music while holding hands. The huge smiles on our faces could be seen for miles — I haven't had this much fun in a really long time.

As the second song ends, we return to the table, only to sip the remainder of our drinks. I hand my empty glass to Rhett and smile cheekily.

He grins at me before taking the cup out of my hand and scooping a little more ice into it. He grabs the vodka bottle and pours an exaggerated amount into my glass, only adding a splash of cranberry.

Perfect.

I see Ford and Katie laughing out of the corner of my eye. I know Ford will make a good husband one day. He always talks about how he'd love to have a wife and a lot of kids. Rhett, on the other hand, is the complete opposite, so if Katie were to get involved with one of them, I would rather it be my brother for *no* other reason than selfishly being ok with her as my in-law.

Rhett hands the drink back to me while sipping on his own. My fingers lightly graze his as I take the glass from him, a warming sensation caresses my body and paints my cheeks, but I brush it off — that drink I just chugged is running through my system, just working its course. I spin around to head back into the crowd when I see a familiar face staring at me from the outside of the dance floor, and I smile as I walk up to him.

"Emilia, right?" Jacob says as he leans in. I nod and smile as I take a sip of my vodka cranberry. "I'm sorry I had to leave so soon last time." He laughs.

"It's fine, don't worry!" I smile and yell over the music.

"You celebrating tonight?" He asks as he points to our VIP section.

"I had a great day at work today, so my brothers and coworker wanted to take me out." I say, cutting to the chase.

"Congrats." He says with a crooked smirk.

God damn, he's so fine. His teeth are pure white, the type of teeth that he probably wore his retainer religiously as a child. They couldn't possibly get any straighter. His eyes are almost a light gray with the shade of blue they are. Sort of like Rhett's, except his reflect the ocean more.

"Do you want to dance?" He asks.

I nod and tell him to hold on one second, only so I can drop my drink off at the table and walk back to him. I hear a remix of *Under The Influence* by Chris Brown fill the room through the speakers which just so happens to be one of my favorite songs. I grab Jacob's hand and spin around, grinding on him with the music as my back lies flat on his chest. He grabs my waist and holds me close to his body. I can't stop smiling. The mix of the alcohol, the day, and now this, I'm on *cloud fucking nine*.

I quickly glance at our table and see Ford and Katie sitting closer together. Her knees touch his as she looks at him with a smile while he speaks. I sway my hips some more as my focus shifts to Rhett with his glass to his lips and his sight... *locked* on me. I narrow my eyes at him in confusion. I roll my hips again and I see his jaw clench tightly. I continue to move side to side, and as I grind on Jacob...again, I see Rhett tighten his jaw. I quickly unlock my gaze from his, thinking it must be a coincidence. Maybe he is looking at something else near me. I dance a bit more before I shift my eyes back at Rhett — his stare, still stuck on me. I roll my hips one more time to test my theory, and sure enough, he clenches again, hard and tight, so the muscles in his jaw practically protrude from the sides of his face.

What in the hell is wrong with him?

I spin and face Jacob before I throw my arms around his neck. He looks into my eyes and smiles.

"What are you doing after this?" He asks me.

"Going home. Are you coming with?" I reply with a grin.

He smiles even bigger and leans in to kiss me softly. I hold my smile until our lips meet and gently brush mine against his. "I'll be right back. I need a drink." I say to him.

"I'll come find you. I need to get mine too." He says before we both part ways.

"Having fun?" I say to the three of them in the booth. Ford now has his arm draped over Katie's leg, and Rhett is still in the same position. Leaning back with his legs parted wide.

"Who's that?" Rhett says as he flicks his head upward with his eyebrows pinched and nods to the direction of the dance floor.

"Jacob. Why?" I ask firmly. Looking at him in utter confusion.

Why the fuck does he care?

"I'm coming to dance!" Katie yells as she darts up, almost spilling her drink. I sip mine again before grabbing her hand and leading her back out. We dance and move to the music. It's more techno sounds booming through the speakers now, so jumping around is the only thing we can think to do.

"You're brother is really nice!" She shouts to me as we move around.

I smile slightly as we continue to dance. Jacob spots me and walks through the crowd, pressing himself behind me again. We all stay on the dance floor for at least three songs before heading back to our table. I invite Jacob to sit with us, and we spend the rest of the night drinking and laughing. Occasionally Rhett and my eyes meet, but I quickly break the gaze as soon as it happens. Somewhere along the line, we had to order a second bottle of Vodka too. My face is feeling hot from the drinks, and the only thing on my mind is getting Jacob in my bed.

"You guys ready to head out?" I ask. Everyone nods, and we flag down our bottle girl to pay the tab. Ford throws down our parent's credit card, and we all finish the last of our drinks. Katie looks incredibly intoxicated, and Ford offers to take her home. Once our tab is paid, Ford and Katie grab an Uber, and Rhett, Jacob, and I walk back to our apartment. I'm not sure what Rhett's issue was, but he seems fine now. He and Jacob have been talking about football for the past thirty minutes, and I'm just trying to keep a clear head and sober up so I can remember tonight. Once we get to the apartment complex, we head upstairs to our floor and walk in the door.

"Here's my home!" I say enthusiastically to Jacob as I stretch my arms to the sides, displaying the living room and kitchen. "And... here's my bedroom." I say as I pull on his hand and lead him into my room. "Night, Rhett!"

As soon as the door closes, I toss my arms around Jacob's neck and dive in, intermixing my lips with his. Moving my tongue inside his mouth as he parts it open for me, flirting his tongue with mine. I reach my hands around and tug on the strings to my top, releasing the straps and letting the silk fall to the floor.

"Shit." He says with a smile as he moves his gaze to my breasts.

I hate to toot my own horn, but for the size of them, they naturally sit a little higher than most. Maybe it's because of my age, but regardless, they're my favorite asset.

I kiss him again and push him closer to my bed as I unbutton my jeans. He slowly backs onto my bed and leans on his elbows as his legs slightly dangle off the side. I pull down my jeans and stand before him in nothing but a thong before I climb on top of him and continue pushing my lips onto his. My heart starts to race, and my breathing deepens. I sit up and open my eyes, the room begins to spin, and I bring my hand to my forehead.

"You okay?" He asks with concern in his voice.

"Yeah," I breathe, "I think — I think I need some water. Can you hold on a second?" I say as the words spill out of my mouth involuntarily. The last thing I want to do is be sick right now.

"Of course." He says, sitting himself up more.

I climb off of him as gently as I can and grab the first thing in my closet to throw on, a small white crop top. *Fuck it*. Ford's not home, and I'm sure Rhett is sleeping already. I quietly open my door and close it behind me before I tiptoe straight into the kitchen as my eyes adjust to the darkness.

"Shit!" I yell in a whisper. "You scared the fuck out of me," I say to Rhett as he sits on a stool by the kitchen island.

"Why are you sitting here...in the dark?" I ask as I move around the island and get a drinking glass from the cupboard.

"I'm not tired." He says flatly, in his gruff voice.

I don't even care that I'm in a thong in front of him right now, my head is spinning, and if I don't have water in three seconds, I *will* pass out.

"You really gonna fuck that guy?" He asks as he raises his eyebrows.

"Excuse me?" I snap, stunned. "Why do you care?" And what's with you giving me dirty looks at the club?" I spout off as I fill up my water glass.

"I wasn't giving you dirty looks?" He questions.

"You guys get to fuck whoever you want, whenever you want. Why is it a problem if I do it?" I scowl. Not giving him a chance to explain anything. I take a large gulp of my water as I see Rhett's eyes fall to my chest. My hard nipples are doing everything they can to ensure they are seen through this shirt. "Are you jealous?!" I ask rather loudly.

"Abso-fucking-lutley not." He snaps back.

"Are you sure?"

"I'm really fucking sure. Do you think that guy in there is going to make you cum? I've got nothing to be jealous of." He laughs. I snap my head back, confused. *Why the fuck would he care?*

I take a second and catch the breath lodged in my throat. I look at Rhett, only in his sweatpants, sitting across from me. His arms are defined with every muscle there could be. He looks tense. More tense than normal. I swallow hard and set my water glass down.

"You don't think he can make me cum?" I ask, testing him, entertaining whatever little game this is that he wants to play.

He shakes his head no as his tongue moves across his teeth with closed lips. I laugh, in disbelief this is even a conversation. I'm drunk and annoyed. I don't know what his fucking problem is. I've never seen him be this way before. I take a small breath to calm my nerves — if he wants to play games, *we'll fucking play them.*

I'm going to fuck Jacob...

and Rhett's going to watch.

Chapter 6

Emilia

I walk back into my room and leave the door slightly ajar. I quickly glance back to try to make out Rhett's figure in the darkness. I see him, his body now shifted around, facing my room directly.

"Come here." I smile at Jacob as he slides to me. I pull him up and position him at the end of my bed, nudging him slightly to fall back. He does and leans himself on his elbows to watch me. I slowly take the hem of my shirt in my hands and lift it over my head. My breasts bounce a little after they are released, my hair slips through the top, and the tousles tickle my back as they fall. I glide my hands up my body and grab onto my breasts, only to massage them gently. Jacob's mouth drops in awe, but in my mind, I want to know if Rhett can see too.

I place my hands on Jacob's thighs and slowly glide them up his jeans until my fingers reach the brass button that keeps everything I want to see hidden. I lift my eyes to him as I unfasten the button and tug at the sides of his pants. He helps me slide them down with his boxers. He's already fully erect, and I smile as I look at him. It's nothing I can't handle. I take him in my hand and slowly drag my tongue up his shaft, wrapping my mouth around him once I get to the tip. I take all of him in my mouth as I bob my head up and down, dragging my tongue with me. I open my eyes and swiftly glance to the left to look out my door. I see Rhett's figure still in place. I close my eyes quickly and continue as Jacob moans slightly. I suck and tease him as his hand falls to the back of my head. He slightly grabs at my hair, and I speed up my rhythm.

"I want to fuck you." He whimpers.

I release my mouth from him and stand up to pull my thong off. He reaches into the back pocket of his jeans and pulls out a condom from his wallet.

"Move back." I breathe as I climb on top of him.

He scoots back as he puts the condom on and licks his fingers, wiping them on me to get me wet. He grabs his cock and fumbles to slip it in until he finds the right angle of my opening. I slide down on him gently and moan, *maybe a little exaggerated*. I roll my hips and throw my head back as I grab onto my left breast — squeezing whatever I can fit in my hand. I rock back and forth as Jacob's hands grab my waist gently. He groans as I lean my body forward to bounce my ass on top of him while his dick slides back and forth in me. I sit up and get off of him slightly, turning around so I face my door.

My open door.

I massage both breasts and bite my bottom lip in a fashion — like I'm some porn star putting on a performance of a lifetime. I continue the same motion back and forth on Jacob as I bring my middle finger to my lips and suck on it slowly before I slide it down to my clit and rub in circular motions. I make sure my legs are spread wide enough and whimper loudly as I work on myself while Jacob lifts his hips higher to plunge into me from below. Each hard thrust makes my breasts bounce and clash together, and I bite my lower lip again with a smirk as I stare into the abyss of darkness, knowing Rhett's figure is still sitting on the stool in the kitchen. I throw my head back and moan, making sure every movement is slightly more exaggerated than the truth. Jacob's plunges become faster, more staggered until I feel him shake. He lets out a strained groan as his thrusts become slower.

That motherfucker. He came already.

A heavy sigh escapes his lips, and I smile, hoping Rhett can see my expression. I exhale loudly to match Jacob, even though my breath is fine, and I slowly move off of him and turn. His hands immediately grab my face as his mouth crushes on mine.

"You're unbelievable." He breathes into me.

I kiss him again quickly and slide off the bed to grab an oversized t-shirt before I walk to my bathroom. I sit on the toilet momentarily with my head in my hand while my elbow rests on my knee. Feeling flustered and unsatisfied all in one.

After I wash my hands, I open my bathroom door and see Jacob sitting on the edge of my bed in just his boxers.

"I hate to do this, but I've got to get up super early in the morning. We can have a sleepover next weekend, though?" I lie with a smile.

"Oh, yeah, of course." He says with a grin as he stands up to grab his jeans. "My phone is right there. Put your number in." He says as he nods while he buttons his pants.

I grab his phone and type it in, smiling as I hand it back. He tucks it away in his back pocket and then pulls his shirt down. He gives me a gentle kiss, still grinning.

"I'll walk you out," I say as we move towards my bedroom door.

He thankfully doesn't seem to notice it's already open before he walks through it. But if I turn on the lamp and he sees Rhett sitting in the direct line of fire, he might think twice about it. I reach for the light and as it flicks on quickly, I hold my breath. The room illuminates, and Rhett... is nowhere to be found.

"I'll call you." He whispers once we get to my front door. I nod, and he plants another kiss on me before he leaves.

I go back to my room and pull out my vibrator from the nightstand, slipping under the covers and taking it with me. I turn it on and moan quietly as the vibrations hit my clit. I press it firmer as I close my eyes and imagine Jacob thrusting into me. He leans down to kiss me and pulls back up. Only it turns into Rhett's face. I spring open my eyes and catch my breath. Clicking my vibrator off and sitting up on my elbows.

What the fuck?

I settle my breathing, then start again. Turning it on and resuming my position. I think of me, holding and sucking Jacob's dick, but then my mind flashes to Rhett, and I don't stop it. I think of him and his face, how sharp his jaw is, and how he looked clenching it at the club. I imagine him grinding his teeth at the thought of me fucking someone else. Then I think of his body. His chest and tattoos. How big his arms are and how his stomach muscles are defined and carved perfectly. I think about the way his v-cut abs on his hips drag down entirely to his cock. *I wonder what it looks like.* I imagine it's big just from the body he has, too much for me to take. I think of him slowly pulling down his shorts at the gym today, and his dick bouncing as they slide off. I moan again as I think of him taking himself in his hand and stroking back and forth until he's about to cum.

Fuck.

That was enough for me. I whimper as my body contracts, and my legs shake as I orgasm. My breathing is rapid as my shaking eventually slows down. I pull the vibrator away from me and shut it off. I lay there, my arms spread out as I try to relax my pulse.

What in the fuck did I just do?

What in the hell was I thinking?

These thoughts are not normal. I've grown up with this man. I've known this man since I was eleven. He's like a brother to me. What am I even doing? I don't have these feelings for Rhett...at least, anymore, and he certainly doesn't have them for me. What have I done? And he's seen me completely naked. *Fucking* someone.

My breathing gets faster as my thoughts come pouring in. I sit up and take deep breaths. Looking over at my vibrator and grabbing it before forcefully shoving it into my drawer. I slap my hands over my face to cover my eyes and groan into them. It'll be fine...maybe Rhett won't say anything to me about it, and we can just forget it ever happened. I'll stop using the fucking vibrator, too, since it assisted in this terrible act.

Yes. It's a plan.

We'll just avoid Rhett and never cum again. Super.

Chapter 7

Rhett

I shouldn't have watched last night, and my dick certainly shouldn't have been throbbing either, but here we are. Mistake after mistake is all I seem to make.

Maybe coming to Chicago wasn't the best idea. It's true I only took a job here because Ford was going to start schooling downtown, but it's not like I have anywhere else to be, regardless. I don't have a home base, and these fuckers are the closest family I have besides my parents, and I don't even speak to my dad.

I lie here on Ford's unbearable pull-out, and I can't even wrap my head around what happened last night — *what the fuck was I thinking?*

I turn over slightly as the metal frame underneath me creaks. This is quite possibly the worst thing I've ever slept on. I'm grateful, nonetheless, but you would think, with how swanky this place is, they would at least provide something between a prison mattress and an actual bed — this is worse.

Ford still isn't back yet, thank God, because I'm not sure how I can explain why I don't want to see Emilia today.

Hey Ford, sorry man, I'm not leaving this room because last night I intently watched your sister blow some guy and then ride him completely naked, and afterward I came into your bedroom and got off just thinking about it.

Yeah — I'd rather not.

I had no fucking business even saying anything, to begin with. But Christ did she have to wear that out of her bedroom? The smallest thong on the planet that her plump ass wholeheartedly swallows and the thinnest white t-shirt that showed me the entire outline of her tits.

Oh god, her tits.

They sit so fucking perfectly.

Jesus, Rhett, get a grip.

I shift my thoughts to what I plan on eating as my stomach growls before I lazily get out of this hell hole of a bed and walk to the bathroom, only to make sure I turn the shower to extra cold. I slide my sweatpants and boxers off and step into the shower. It only takes me a second to adjust to the shock of the chill, but I need it — anything to forget last night.

It's not like I want to replay Emilia's full lips wrapped around some fucking douchebag. Or that I want to think of the way her breasts bounced every time she slammed down on him.

I just...want to forget it.

Do I really?

No.

Do I have to?

Yes.

But the way my cock is throbbing right now just thinking about her says otherwise.

I turn to adjust the water temperature back to normal, If I'm going to give in, I might as well be comfortable. I place my hands on the shower wall as the hot water hits my back. I slowly take my hand and wrap it around my cock as I stroke up and down my length, gripping tight enough for me to imagine it's her mouth. I don't know if she could take all of me, but *fuck* I want to see her try. I work harder and faster on myself as I focus on the head of my cock now. I want to see Emilia beg for me. Crave me, the way I want her right now, so I imagine her kneeling in front of me as she takes every inch of me inside of her mouth. I think about coming on her face — all over her forehead, the bridge of her nose, and down to her chin. I want to paint her pretty fucking features white and watch her lick it off her pouty lips. I grip my cock harder as it swells and grunt as I feel my heart pound. I can feel the pressure rise as a surge of electricity hits me, and my cum pumps out. I moan as I squeeze tight, pushing the last bit I can out as I exhale the long-winded breath I was holding once I feel the release and place both of my hands back on the shower wall as I calm my breathing.

Christ. This has got to be the last time.

I can't do this anymore, and I know it.

I turn myself around and let the blood pump through my body as I move the shower handle once more and feel the sharpness of the cool water again.

Most of the shower is spent actually washing. The other half — *besides the totally fucked up masturbation* — is spent immobile, standing underneath the water as it runs down my face and body while I contemplate every other appalling thing I have done since coming to Chicago, including getting jealous at the club, *over her*.

As soon as I'm dressed, I already know the plan is to stay in the bedroom. I'll just blame it on the hangover tomorrow. I prop myself up on my bed *if you can even call it that*, and click the TV on while I reach for my phone. My first text is to Ford, only to ensure he's alive, and then to my mom before I order delivery to let her know about my job. I'm thankful for her. Unlike Emilia and Ford's parents, my mother was around most of the time, it was just my father that was not.

The entire day goes by, and I miraculously don't see Emilia. Her bedroom door closed once before mine opened, and I thought our Uber Eats might have come at the same time, but lucky for me, hers must have come first. Ford returned home in the afternoon but looked like he had gotten the worst night's sleep. *He must have been up all night with what's her face.* She seemed nice enough, and Emilia really likes her, so I hope it works out for them. While Ford slept nearly the rest of the night, I vegged out on my couch bed.

I can only hope tomorrow goes as smoothly and that my big mouth doesn't get me in trouble. And lord knows if she's wearing anything *white*, I'll be back in that cold shower tomorrow morning.

Chapter 8

Emilia

I slept through all of Sunday, only getting out of bed to grab my Uber Eats from the door. A mix of a raging hangover and my self-loathing kept me there, both pretty present the whole day. I'm off work today, but it's Ford's first day of class. My alarm just went off, and I should at least leave my bedroom for more than ten minutes today. I sit up and dangle my feet off the side of my bed, stretching until I feel loose enough. Then I walk straight into my closet. I grab an ivory-thin strap sports bra and matching biker shorts before I walk out of my room, rubbing the drowsiness out of my eye as I near the kitchen. The sunlight from the early morning seeps in from the large windows in the living room, covering all of the open space our apartment has to offer. Casting a warm glow throughout that touches every piece of furniture we have.

"Good morning." I say to Ford as he stands in front of the coffee maker.

"Morning." He replies, his voice low and gruff from his sleep.

"What time is your first class?" I ask him as I grab a coffee mug from beside his head.

"In, like, an hour." He says as he glances at the clock on the stove.

"Morning." Rhett says from behind, his voice even deeper than Ford's, still riddled with the gruffness of his sleep too.

"Morning." Ford and I both say.

I turn around to face Rhett for the first time since the other night, but instead of his face, my eyes somehow fall to his waistline. His gray sweatpants are pulled down slightly, and his white briefs show through the top. I quickly snap my gaze back to his eyes which are thankfully looking at Ford. Rhett brings his arms up to his head, his stomach muscles stretching with him, his biceps flex lightly as he presses his palms into his eyes to rub them. I swallow a dry gulp and move over to start my coffee, placing the pod in the holder and closing the lid.

"How long did you stay at Katie's?" I ask Ford as he sits on the chair in the living room. I didn't see or talk to him yesterday, so it's my time to catch up.

"I didn't come home until like three yesterday." He says.

"Don't like...hurt her, okay? I can see a friendship between us and would at least like to have one friend in this city." I say, my tone growing softer as I think of the words coming out of my mouth.

"Oh, you have two friends Em. That Jake guy seems nice?" Rhett chimes in with a grin.

"His name is Jacob, and he's *very* nice." I snark.

"I kind of like her," Ford says as he sips his coffee, disregarding Rhett and I's little spat.

"Really?" I ask excitedly as I bring my coffee to the living room and sit with the boys.

"Yeah. She was really sick after the club and begged me to stay, so I slept on the couch. We hung out most of yesterday, just talking about random shit." He says casually.

"You what?" I ask, in shock. Ford is not usually known to be a gentleman and certainly not known to just sleep on a girl's couch.

"Yeah." He chuckles. "We didn't even have sex."

"What?" Rhett asks, surprised.

You and me both, buddy.

Ford laughs as he gets up. "I gotta get ready." He says as he walks to his room and closes the door.

"You think he's in love?" Rhett asks me.

"Sounds like it."

"Sounds miserable." He smirks.

Moments of silence pass, and the air between us grows so heavy and thick you couldn't even cut it with the sharpest knife.

"So, did you have a good night with Jake?" He asks as he locks in my gaze.

"Jacob. And yes, I did." I tilt my head and grin with purpose.

"That's good...but he still didn't make you cum." He smiles as he stands up and walks between the coffee table and me. The top of his boxers is directly in my sight as he moves past, and the veins in his stomach that lead down under his pants scream at me to look at them. I quickly shift my gaze to his eyes, only to see him looking down at me. He walks into Ford's room and shuts the door. My face grows warm and flushed, and I can feel the thumping of my heartbeat through my chest. I snap out of it quickly as the bedroom door opens again. This time, it's Ford.

"I won't be home until like five today. Can you make something good for dinner? It's my first day Em." He begs, half kidding — half not.

"Just think about what you want and text me later. Good luck." I say. He smiles before walking into the foyer. No sooner does he disappear the front door shuts.

I sigh and grab the remote, turn on the TV, and flip through the channels. I hear the shower start from Ford's bathroom, and my mind races with thoughts of what Rhett is doing in there. I turn the TV up a little louder to block out the sound of the running water, probably hitting Rhett's naked body. I continue to watch Bravo while sipping my coffee when I hear the faint sound of his voice. I turn the tv down a bit and listen closer before I stand up and walk to the bedroom door, placing my ear on it. I hear the water running still and *some* sound. I feel that maybe investigating the situation could be helpful. For all I know, he slipped and fell. I twist the doorknob quietly and push it open, and my eyes land directly at the bathroom door that isn't shut fully. I take large steps, tiptoeing on the wood to not make a sound. I peer through the crack in the bathroom door and see Rhett through the glass shower, rubbing his cock back and forth with one hand while the other hand holds him up by the wall. His moans are low and gruff, and my eyes are locked on him. He twists his hand up and down the length. He's everything I imagined...and more. I take another step to get my footing right when the wood floor creaks. He stops and stands up straight immediately.

"Emilia." He demands.

I don't move. I stay as still as possible.

"Emilia, come here." He says sternly.

I stand up straighter and open the door fully. Rhett gets out of the shower as I walk in, his cock still fully erect, and the water droplets coat his skin with individual pellets.

"Emilia, we can't do this." He says as he grabs a towel from the rack.

"Do what?" I ask as my heart pounds.

"This." He says as he wraps the towel around him and points between us back and forth. "I'm sorry. I shouldn't have watched you the other night," he takes a step closer, minimizing the space between us. "We can't...do this." He says slowly. His body is still dripping wet, wearing only the towel around his waist and his gold chain.

"Why?" I ask as I look up at him, my eyes begging for him. The word spewed out of me like lava. I didn't mean to say it.

I know why.

"Emilia, you wouldn't like the way I fuck anyways." He groans.

My breaths quicken as fast as my pulse — rapid and rigid. I don't know what he means, but every piece of my aching soul wants to.

"You don't want me?" I ask, my tone soft and innocent.

"I never said that." He says roughly as he takes another step towards me, our bodies nearly touching.

I take a deep breath.

What the fuck am I doing?

"You're right. We shouldn't do this. I agree." I say, slightly stammering. I turn to walk out the door, and he grabs my arm immediately. My body jerks back to face him as his grip remains tight.

"Don't think for one second I don't want to fuck you. I've thought about it for years. I can't. *We* can't." He voices.

My breath becomes audibly louder. It's harder to breathe quietly when I need so much air.

"Why won't I like having sex with you?" I ask as my hand lifts to touch the towel on his hip, ready to pull it off.

"Because it's not sex, Emilia. It's fucking, *hard*." He says, his voice thick and low.

His words cease in my head, only momentarily before I tug at his towel, releasing it from his hand. His cock is semi-hard, hanging, and still lengthy.

"Emilia." He warns. "I'm telling you, it's not how you want to be fucked."

"You don't know what I want." I say as my body lunges closer and my lips crash onto his like a rogue wave hitting a ship.

I don't even know what the fuck I want.

I know how he treats women — like they're his fuck toy he can throw away when he's done. His ideas of marriage and relationships significantly differ from mine, and here I am...craving him like he's my favorite fucking meal.

His tongue dips into my mouth, and I run mine back into his at the same time. He grabs my waist and pushes me to the wall behind me, making sure my back slams flat against it. He groans as his mouth moves with mine. His lips are soft and plush — wet with his tongue.

"Fuck." He moans as his hand meets my jaw. He grabs tightly on my face as his lips part with mine. "Emilia." He whispers with sorrow in his eyes.

What is he going to do to me?

I look at him and breathe heavily into his mouth. I nod slightly, hoping this lets him know I want him to keep going. His lips collide with mine again as he lets go of my face and forcefully yanks my sports bra down. The sound of it ripping shoots both of our gazes down to look only for a moment before his mouth is back on mine. I grab his cock tightly and wrap my hand around it as much as possible, failing to get my fingers to touch. I keep the same grip as I stroke his length. He nearly pulsates beneath my palm as he grows even harder by the second. A moan escapes from him before he bites my bottom lip with force. I whimper slightly at the sting of it and nudge his face away from mine, only to take my bra off completely, pulling it over quickly around my head before my shorts come off next. It's not like I have a plan; my rational thinking has flown out the window a long time ago. I kneel in front of him, not knowing what else to do.

A sigh breaks free from his throat while he sweeps my hair up and bundles it into one hand for some makeshift ponytail. My eyes flutter to his immediately, and I glimpse his sinister grin on top of his clenched jaw. I grab a hold of his cock and lift it, only to drag my tongue on the underside along his length, just until I get to the tip. I keep our eyes locked together as I begin to suck and sweep only the tip with my tongue. He lets out a low groan as I try to take him fully in my mouth, failing to get close to his stomach. I stick my tongue out as far as I can while I suck him, making sure to run my lips with it each time. I break my eye contact away only for a moment to adjust my hands when he tugs at the back of my head.

"Look at me." He groans as his grip remains tight on my hair, holding a fistful of my locks.

He pushes my head onto him, shoving himself as far down my throat as he can. My eyes widen as he thrusts into me repeatedly, causing me to gag. He moans louder as he releases slightly, letting me catch my breath while his thick cock still resides in my mouth. He only gives me a moment before pushing my head into him again, slamming his dick into the back of my throat over and over until my gagging is the only noise filling the bathroom. He tugs at the back of my hair, still in the ponytail he made, and makes sure that I'm still looking directly into his eyes. His hips thrust into me as his cock continually hits my uvula, and I squeeze onto my thumb as the only trick I know to stop my gag reflex. As the water wells up in my eyes, my vision becomes blurry but not enough to where I can't see another smile sweep across his face before he holds my head at the base of him, keeping me there without oxygen for three or four seconds. His cock — now directly lodged in my throat, is the only thing blocking my windpipe. He pulls out of my mouth completely, and I gasp for air and cough as my saliva runs down my chin and to the side of my face until it lands on the floor.

"Good girl." He says with a low groan.

I only take enough time to catch my breath slightly before I wrap my lips around him again, stroking him back and forth as my tongue glides against him. He doesn't waste any time before he shoves his cock to the back of my throat again, fucking my face as hard as he can. He pulls out quickly with a loud grunt, and in an instant, his right hand swoops to the side of my face and slaps me. The biting pain sears at my cheek and jaw where he hit, and I'm too stunned to even calibrate what just happened. I take him back in my mouth and push further to the back of my throat. It's better if I do it, so I can somewhat breathe. He moans as his head falls back slightly, but only briefly before his eyes are locked back on mine.

"You're so fucking pretty with my cock in your mouth." He groans as he pulls out of me again and bends over to be eye level with me.

It only takes another moment before my head is yanked back again, and another strike from his palm hits my face. I whimper from the force, and my eyes well again with tears. Not only from the continual gagging but from the new addition of pinching pain of what I'm sure is a bright red mark left on my cheek.

Without hesitation, he lifts me from under my arms and picks me up. My legs wrap around his waist as he carries me out of the bathroom, only taking a few steps before throwing me onto the bed. I brace myself up from my elbows to watch him as he kneels at the edge of the bed and forces himself between my legs, burying his face right in my pussy. The immediate sensation of his mouth sucking on my clit and the stubble from his face scratching all the right places result in some sort of cry and grunt unleashing from my lips.

He places his hand firmly on my lower stomach as his tongue traces my slit only for a moment before two fingers from his other hand shove inside me. I cry out as he sucks and flicks my clit with his tongue, pushing his fingers deep inside of me and curling them upward. The feeling presses on something I've never experienced before, and I scream while my legs shake uncontrollably. The sounds of my wetness and him sucking fill my ears as I prop myself on an elbow again and look at him, his eyes on me and his mouth wrapped around my entire pussy.

I see it in his eyes, the fire, like how he's going to fuck up my entire life...and I'm going to let him.

"I'm gonna cum." I whimper as he keeps a steady pace, thrusting his fingers in and pausing when he's deep inside to curl the tips of them.

My pussy contracts as my hips grind on his face. His moans can faintly be heard over mine when I finish my orgasm. My legs close shut on his head and I place my hand on his head to push him off — too sensitive after coming to have my clit touched again. His mouth stays locked on me as he keeps his strength like cement. He continues thrusting his fingers deep inside of me with his mouth working at the same time. His eyes glance up at mine as my mouth stays dropped. I moan while my eyes roll back, and he pushes my legs up to my chest, plunging his fingers inside me, deeper and deeper. He lifts his mouth from my pussy as he thrusts harder, only a couple of times before pulling out, my wetness spraying in the air. He goes back in, hitting that same fucking spot as I cry out. He pulls his fingers out quickly as I spray him again. The droplets hit his stomach like he ran through a fucking sprinkler... and for the first time in my life, I think I'm squirting.

"Fuck yeah, just like that, you can do it, baby." He groans as he pushes in again, curling his fingers several times before pulling them out of me. I moan, feeling like I have to pee, and I hold my breath as he continues. I feel like I'm losing all control — I have to give in. I can't hold it any longer. I groan as I relax and shut my eyes, releasing all tension in my body. His fingers go faster, still pulling out, except this time I'm soaked. I feel whatever it is just pour out of me, and my screams fill the room. He moans loudly as he flattens his hand out and vigorously rubs it over my pussy, spraying both of us with my gushing liquid.

I whimper and look at him, a jaw-dropped grin stuck on his face as he quickly lifts his hand and slaps my pussy — stinging my throbbing clit. The feeling sends my mind into a fucking spiral. I've never experienced this before...with anyone.

I want him inside of me.

Right fucking now.

He grabs me tightly, tossing me further to the middle of the bed as he climbs on.

"Fuck." He groans as he grabs my face and plants a kiss on me.

His grip remains firm, squeezing me so hard my lips pucker. The brilliance in his eyes pierces through mine as he nestles his cock between my thighs and keeps his mouth close to mine. He releases his grasp on my face only to swat at it again, grinning at the same time. The ends of my lips curl upwards in some half-assed smile, and he grabs his cock and rubs it on my pussy only once before shoving it right into my entrance, forcing me to take every inch of him immediately. I cry out. It feels like he's in my fucking stomach. He lifts my legs with one hand as he thrusts into me, filling me fully with him every time. He grips my breast hastily and pinches my nipple, sending a shocking sting through me as he continues to toy with it.

He lets go of my legs only to part them further and grabs the back of my neck forcefully, lifting my head to his, putting me in some sort of crunch while he pounds into my pussy. He grunts as the sweat glistens and rolls down his arms, perfectly coating each line and every shade of his tattoos — making the black pigment shine and radiate from his tanned skin. I wrap my hands around the back of his neck, threading my fingers together to hold on as he relentlessly thrusts. He brings his hand to my throat, pinning me back down to the bed as he firmly squeezes, almost blocking my entire windpipe. My mouth hangs open, trying to suck in any air I can while his lips press on mine again, only for a moment before he draws back and spits into my mouth. The realization hits me too late when his lips are back on mine, and my tongue is coated with his thick saliva. It's only for a moment until our spit is interchanged with each other, our tongues rolling around against one another, and our breathing in sync with the most chaotic rhythm.

He grabs my breast forcefully as his head falls to my chest, sweeping my nipple into his mouth as he flicks and bites at it. I tilt my head to look at him and watch as his tongue circles around my taut pink bud, occasionally tugging it between his lips. I know I'm close to coming again and I whimper as it nears.

"Not yet." He breathes into my face before pulling out of me and flipping me over on my stomach.

He takes hold of my hips, dragging me toward him before he thrusts into my pussy from behind.

I feel him hitting that same fucking spot his fingers were just moments ago. He releases his grasp with only one hand as he slaps my ass with force. I grunt at the stinging pain, and he does it again. The echoing of the clap fills my ears, and another biting pain reeks through my entire body as I gasp for air.

"Come here, baby." He groans as he fists my hair with one hand and jerks my neck back, bringing my body flush with his.

Slowing down his rhythm, he reaches his hand to cup my breast, squeezing as he keeps a firm hold on my hair, nearly pulling it from the root. He runs his tongue along my neck before biting my earlobe. I turn my face slightly as his tongue thrusts into my mouth. Our lips, uneven from his continual pounding into me. He releases my breast and firmly grabs my throat again, choking me while my mouth stays on his. We moan into each other while I feel him fill me — his cock, throbbing inside me.

"Fuck." He groans in between our mouths colliding. His thrusts remain deep and slow as he grips me tightly.

He releases me from his hold, pushing me to my knees again as his grip falls to my hips. His tight hold on me hurts, but the discomfort intertwined with the pleasure overpowers any feelings of true agony. He plunges into me faster, and my cries become uneven, changing tone with every thrust.

"I'm coming." I cry out, and he moans, slapping his hand on my ass once more before gripping my cheeks and spreading them, making it easier for him to enter me. My pussy contracts around him, and my legs shake as my position becomes unsteady.

"Cum on my cock, baby, cum on my cock." He groans with gritted teeth as I whimper. "Holy fuck, you're so tight."

"Fuck!" I drag out in a moan as my orgasm continues.

"That's it baby...that's it. God, you're gonna make me cum. Oh fuck, you're gonna make me cum." He moans as his thrusts become faster.

My whimpering subsides only for a moment to hear him. He grunts as he plunges deep inside of me, my wetness clapping against him with every thrust. He sighs as he pounds one last time, holding me still with every inch of him inside of me. I feel his cock throbbing as the last bit of him drains, and for the first time, the realization hits me.

He wasn't even wearing a condom.

Chapter 9

Emilia

This must be what the men feel like every time I kick them out after sex. Alone, breathing hard, and in pure ecstasy. Albeit, it doesn't feel great to have the person who just fucked you raw stay in the bathroom forever while your lying on a bed, cum dripping out of you, and completely naked, like I am in this very moment.

I hear the bathroom door open, and I shift my head to look. Rhett is entirely dressed already.

"You didn't wear a condom," I say softly.

"I know." He says as he puts his watch on.

"And you came inside of me..." I say, enunciating everything, trying to get him to understand the problem.

I slowly get off the bed and see Ford's silver comforter completely drenched. A large wet spot soaks through the comforter on the right side, and an even bigger wet spot soaks through right in front of me. I grab the end and yank it off his bed, the pillows on top falling to the side as I do.

"Hello?" I snark as I look at him.

"Emilia, we can't do this again." He says as he looks at me, his lips pressed shut. "I'll get you a Plan B when I go out." He finishes.

I scoff.

The fucking nerve of him.

But should I expect anything less? It's Rhett — only cares about himself, and his feelings, no one else's.

I knew it.

And I still put myself in this position.

"Was I not good enough, Rhett? Is that what it is?" I lash out as I wrap the bedspread up in my hands aggressively. Shielding my naked body from him.

"I don't fuck girls more than once, Emilia. Too many feelings involved. You keep fucking the same person, someone, somewhere is going to catch feelings. I don't do that. You're no exception." He says, not even looking me in the fucking eye anymore.

I click my tongue and nod my head. "There he is. Same old fucking Rhett." I smirk, so pissed off I could scream.

I storm out of the bedroom and throw the bedspread in the wash tucked in a closet in the foyer, tossing in an ungodly amount of detergent. I walk back to my room and see Rhett in the kitchen out of the corner of my eye — not even looking his way before I slam my door shut. I swallow hard, standing in the middle of my room, and then it happens. The misery I was holding in the center of my chest flows right from my eyes and streams down my cheeks. I suck in my bottom lip and bite down hard to not make a sound. I'm not sure what hurts worse... the physical pain from how rough he was or being treated like a fucking whore.

I stand here, alone and naked, crying like some lunatic, before I gather myself together and take a deep breath. I walk to my bathroom and start my shower before looking at myself in the mirror. My hair is mangled, and my left cheek is as bright as a maraschino cherry. I turn my body and pull at my skin lightly to observe the damage done to my ass. It still pings with pain, and almost the entire surface of one cheek is nearly the same color red. I wince as I touch it lightly before I walk to my shower and graze my fingers under the droplets to feel the temperature before I get in. I spend some moments just letting the water fall on my head as I shut my eyes. The blood courses through my veins and every place there is a heartbeat in my body, it's nearly crawling out of my skin.

I can't even process what just happened.

I mean, do I even *want* to have sex with the man again after the pain I was put in?

Yes.

No.

No, Emilia, you do not.

And what kind of aftercare was that? Sure, I go into the bathroom and clean up, but god damn, I'm a little nicer when I kick someone to the curb afterward. He knows me, *well,* at that…don't I deserve some kind of special treatment?

No.

No, Emilia, you do not.

You are no exception.

I spend at least fifteen minutes standing in the shower before leaving. Once I'm dry, I walk into my room, and my eyes fall directly to my bed. My white sports bra and biker shorts lay perfectly pressed on my bed. *That mother fucker.*

I look through my closet and grab a tank top and sweat pants before I yank a zip-up sweatshirt off the hanger. It's my day off, and I don't feel like wearing a bra, but I've got to go to the pharmacy now and make sure I'm not growing the spawn of Satan inside of me. I want children someday, lots of them, but not now, and certainly not with him. I jerk open my bedroom door and walk to the kitchen. Out of the corner of my eye, I see Rhett sitting on the couch watching TV. I open the refrigerator to see what I need. Since I'll be out, I might as well get groceries. Which reminds me —

EMILIA: How are your classes?
What do you want for dinner?

FORD: Stupid. Can you make that thing with the noodles and the cheese, but it's like flat noodles?

EMILIA: Lasagna?

FORD: Yes. Please.

I grab my keys from the counter and walk into the foyer before I slam the front door shut.

I walk to the nearest pharmacy and pay fifty fucking dollars for the pill. On the way home, I swing into the market to grab what I need for dinner. This is all for Ford tonight, none for Rhett, and I'll tell him that too.

I get back home and walk in, the apartment is empty, and I take a breath to relax. I unload the groceries before I take the Plan B out of the brown paper bag of shame. I set it on the island and turn around to grab a wine glass from the cupboard. I've never actually taken one of these, so my anxiety is through the roof — I need to calm my nerves, and the only vice I have here is wine. I pour my Sauvignon Blanc into the stemmed glass and swish it around a couple of times before taking a sip. I lean my elbows on the counter and observe the plastic sealed package from front to back.

Emergency Contraceptive, huh?

I've been on birth control since I was fifteen but this, this is certainly an emergency. I grab scissors and cut open the package after failing to pull it apart with my fingers. I push the pill out of the center and read the card further as I take another sip of wine.

Take as soon as possible, it says — twice.

I get the hint and pop it in my mouth as I hear the door open. I chug the pill down with my wine and place the glass in the sink before Rhett walks into the kitchen.

"I already got one," I say flatly as I see the familiar brown paper bag in his hands. "You can save that one for your next whore."

"Emilia." He says sternly.

I ignore him and crumple up the bag and plastic pieces together before throwing them away.

"Can you listen to me, please?" He says as he sits on the barstool.

I tilt my eyes up with a clenched jaw and give him a hostile glare.

"I told you we shouldn't do it. I warned you. But it happened, and it's done with." He says in his low voice.

I don't respond.

"Emilia, it was great. Your body...you...everything about you is fucking insane. You're perfect, Emilia. But we can't do it again. That's all. Please don't be upset with me."

I swallow dryly and breathe through my nose. "Okay." I say with the best poker face I can slap on before I turn around to fish my wine glass out of the sink and pour a second drink.

I hear Rhett sigh before taking the brown paper bag to his room, and I close my eyes for a moment and take a deep breath. It still doesn't make me feel any better about the situation. All it makes me want to do is fuck him again. Between the fact that I *can't* fuck him and the fact that it was the best sex I've ever had in my life, I can't stop my mind from veering.

The washing machine buzzes and startles me slightly. I grab my wine glass and phone from the island and move the bedspread into the dryer. I sit on the couch once I'm done, and only three seconds of relaxation pass before my phone dings.

JACOB FROM BAR: Can I take you out to dinner tomorrow?

This is the fifth text this man has sent between yesterday and today, and I've only replied to one. My mind has been elsewhere, but maybe I should give him a chance. He seems nice enough. Nicer than Rhett, at least, and that's what I need.

EMILIA: That sounds fun. I have plans tomorrow already. What about the next day?

JACOB FROM BAR: Perfect. I'll pick you up at 6:30, then.

I already told the guys yesterday over text that we could go out tomorrow night for a celebration of Rhett's first day at work. That was, of course, before he fucked my brains out and left me like a hooker without pay.

I glance at the time and decide I should start making dinner. This is one of my favorite recipes that Elizabeth taught me and one of Ford's favorite comfort meals.

"Need any help?" Rhett says as he comes out of the bedroom.

"Sure," I say as I slide a bowl next to me. "You can mix these." I push the cheese-filling ingredients to him.

He doesn't bat an eye and gets to work right away. I can't say this isn't fucking awkward because the man was choking me with his cock an hour ago, but it might be a good thing if we just act like this never happened.

Except that my fucking brain doesn't want to forget.

I look at his stubble, the stubble that felt so good scratching and poking between my legs, neck, and face. His lips, how soft they were…almost like they were melting in my fucking mouth. We moved together so effortlessly, our tongues never *not* in the same rhythm. The tattoos on his arms, how they glistened with the sweat he worked up from pounding my pussy endlessly without so much of a rest or break.

"You okay?" He says as I focus my vision, realizing he's starring directly at me.

"Mhm." I nod my head as I quickly turn to face forward and start on the meat sauce.

"When does your article come out?" He asks.

"Five days." I say with a soft grin while I drain the noodles.

"Where can I buy like…six copies?"

"Why do you want six copies?"

"Because it's your article Em. It's really fucking cool." He says as he slides the cheese mixture bowl my way.

I let out a small gasp, *quiet enough for him not to hear* and smile. I wish he wasn't being nice. It would be much easier to forget about his perfect cock when he's an asshole.

"Help me layer this," I say as I move the pan between us. "Sauce, noodles, cheese. Got it?"

"Sauce, noodles, cheese. Check." He says with a smirk that exposes a dimple.

Fuck.

Why have I never noticed that?

We continue to layer until the pan is filled, then cover it with foil before I place it in the oven.

"Oh shit." I say after I close the oven door. "Ford's bedding." I wipe my hands on a towel before I start to dart off to the dryer.

"I did it already." Rhett stops me. "It's on, just how it was before."

I turn around to walk back to the stove. "Thank you." I smile.

Rhett and I make ourselves useful by cleaning the kitchen while waiting for the lasagna to be done. After Ford texted he was on his way home — we set out wine for me and scotch for the boys at each plate on the island. Rhett lit a candle for a little dazzle in the center, too.

"Perfect." He laughs as the flame sears. He's proud of his table setting, as he should be.

"Is dinner done yet?" Ford calls jokingly from the foyer.

"Waiting on you!" I tease back as he enters the kitchen.

"Oh my god, it smells so good." He says.

"I helped!" Rhett chimes in, grinning from ear to ear.

"Thanks, buddy." Ford chuckles as he fist-bumps Rhett.

"Sit, sit, tell us all about it." I say as I wave my hands to his seat before I scoop them each a perfectly square piece of lasagna from the pan.

"It was good. I mean, physics was stupid, and so was math." He says and then shovels pasta into his mouth. "How was your guys' day?" He asks while he chews.

I swallow a breath, caught off guard by the question.

"It was okay. I didn't do much." I say.

"It was fine, I just didn't do anything." Rhett says at nearly the same time.

Way to go, everyone. Nice job at keeping it cool and calm.

We eat together, just like old times, and thankfully the rest of dinner goes without a hitch. I even managed to only think of Rhett spitting in my mouth twice through it all.

I would certainly call that *a success*.

Chapter 10
Emilia

"She's alive!" I joke to Katie as she walks into work with sunglasses framing her face instead of her regular ones. She plops her large tote bag on her desk and falls into her chair, grunting once her butt hits the seat.

"I'm still hungover." She groans. "I'm not drinking for another month, I swear to god." She says as she half-ass raises her left hand and crosses her heart with her right one. Her fingertips not visible from her completely oversized hoodie.

"On Christ, Emilia." She solidifies her promise.

"Why didn't you call off today?" I laugh.

"Free food. And Kathy's been on my ass — we really need to get the graphics done for your article. Do you have any time today or tomorrow?"

"Can we do it over drinks?" I facetiously ask.

She tilts her chin down so I can see the tops of her eyes peek through her sunglasses as she raises her eyebrows up and down in agreement. I laugh and we both get started on work. Only forty minutes go by of us actually doing anything productive before she dives into talking about Ford.

"He's so nice, and I'm sorry, I know you don't want to hear this, but god damn, is he so fine." She giggles like a schoolgirl.

I roll my eyes with a smile, of course, it's gross hearing how 'fine' he is, but I am dancing a little inside at the thought of them two. "And I told my sister about Rhett. He's hot too. Is he seeing anyone?"

A pit forms in the center of my stomach, like a sinkhole that plummets cars and houses down into the void. The thought of Rhett's sexcapades never crossed my mind. He won't fuck *me* again, that doesn't mean he won't fuck anyone else.

"Rhett doesn't do relationships." I firmly say. "He's more of a...fuck 'em once and leave kind of guy."

She crinkles her nose up, a good indication she doesn't like that for her sister.

Don't worry. I don't like that for me either right now.

"What are you doing tonight?" She asks me after some silence.

"It's Rhett's first day at work. We like to celebrate our wins often," I smile. "So we're taking him out to a fancy restaurant tonight. Want to come?" I ask as I lean into her with a cheesy grin. I don't mind playing matchmaker with her and my brother. It might actually be a little amusing.

"That sounds fun! Which restaurant? And how fancy are we talking?" She asks.

"Eleven Park. I'm going to wear a silk slip from Balmain, and I think the boys are wearing suits."

"Shit, I don't think I have anything that fancy."

"Come over after work! We will get ready together. I'm sure I have something you can wear." I smile.

She nods, and we finish the rest of our day *actually* getting work done.

"Okay. Let's get to work." I say as I lead us into my bedroom. Katie sits on my bed while I riffle through my closet, pulling out every designer dress my mother bought me in hopes of making up for her lack of presence.

"What about this?" I say as I hold up a slinky Valentino dress.

"Wow." She says as she stands up and touches the fabric.

"Go try it on." I smile and tilt my chin up towards my bathroom.

She grins shyly before taking it from me and walking into my bathroom. I sit on my bed, replacing her seat, and wait for her to come out.

"Holy shit." I say with a jaw-dropped smile the second the door opens again. "You look amazing, Katie!" I stand up and grab her arms while I turn her to the side to observe the back. "It fits you perfectly."

"This is gorgeous. I'm so nervous about wearing it." She says as she looks down at the dress and runs her hands along the sides of it.

"Why! Don't be silly."

"I've never worn anything designer before. I see it all of the time at Thirty8, on the shelves and in the fashion closets, but I've never actually *worn* any of it."

"Well how about owning it? It's yours now. I don't want it."

"Absolutely not." She demands. "This is like...a two thousand dollar dress, Emilia."

"It was four thousand. I don't want it, Katie, it's yours."

She laughs in disbelief. "There's no way I'm keeping this."

"Fine, I'll just throw it away."

"You wouldn't." She snaps.

"I would." I smile mischievously.

She mulls it over, bringing herself back into my bathroom and looking at herself in the mirror, turning from side to side to admire it at every angle. She grins largely, then turns to me with a wide smile.

"Thank you." She says softly.

I hear the front door shut and walk out of my bedroom to say hello to Ford.

"I invited Katie tonight. I hope that's fine." I say as he walks into the kitchen.

"Of course. God, I can't wait to see her. I've been thinking about her like crazy." He says as he sets his backpack on the counter.

"She's here." I mouth to him. He quickly snaps his mouth shut and pulls his lips in. *God forbid a woman hears how smitten a guy is over her.*

I head back to my room and swipe my phone open to play Spotify before I set it down on my bathroom counter.

"I've got like three different foundation colors we can mix for you." I say while Post Malone blasts through the tiny speakers on my iPhone.

"You're like a little Sephora." She laughs.

After we find her perfect shade, I hear the front door shut again, *must be Rhett*. I debate for a moment whether I should run out and see how his first day went or play it cool and stay put. It only takes a moment for me to decide that playing it cool was never really my thing.

I drop the makeup brush in my hand and dart out of my room like those suburban moms that fast-walk their babies in strollers. "How was your first day?" I ask excitedly as soon as he's in my line of sight. He smiles when his eyes lock with mine.

"It was really good." He says with a grin. I press my lips together and try to take my mind off the fact that his tattoos look fifty times hotter against his dirty white t-shirt and jeans. Or that his tanned skin looks even darker with the dirt and dust layered over it.

"Reservations are in an hour." Seems to be the only thing I can spit out.

"Thank god. I'm starving." He says before I turn around and walk back into my room. I close my eyes for a moment before a flash of me lifting Rhett's work shirt floods my mind — the veins just on the lower pit of his stomach hypnotize me. His abs show as I lift it higher and over his head before my mouth —

"Do you have eyelash glue?" My thoughts are abruptly interrupted by Katie.

"Yep, let me find it." I say as I move closer to her and dig through another makeup bag of mine.

We finish getting ready, and she zips my dress up in the back before I find her heels to match.

"Should we see if the boys are done?" I ask as she puts the last shoe on.

She nods and stands up straight before we walk out of my room together. Ford is in the kitchen, his dress shirt half buttoned and half tucked in.

"Wow, Katie." He says as he glances between her and the towel draped around the stove he's wiping his hands on. "You look gorgeous." He smiles.

Rhett walks out of the bedroom, pulling the sleeve of his suit jacket down so it lays perfectly by his wrist — just covering up the last bit of his tattoos. I try extremely hard to keep my jaw locked tight, so it doesn't fall open unintentionally. His clean white shirt underneath is left open from the first two buttons, just enough to see his sun-tanned skin on his chest and his gold chain. The prominent stubble on his face is short and freshly trimmed, especially over his top lip, and I wish I could know what that feels like between my thighs.

"You girls look nice." Rhett says to Katie and me.

"So do you boys." I reply. Pushing my tongue to my cheek to keep from saying anything more.

I miss the days when I would look at Rhett and see nothing. I'd see that same fourteen-year-old boy who used to shoot me with BB guns for fun. I would see the sixteen-year-old who would flip me off from the front seat of his car since my brother always called shotgun. I'd see the eighteen-year-old who burnt a frozen pizza after us three stayed on the beach all day without eating a damn thing. Time was simple and carefree.

But I've grown.

We've grown.

Together.

"Let me grab my belt, then we can go." Ford says as he pushes past Rhett and me to get into his room.

"I like that dress." Rhett whispers in my ear. His words send a hot wave through my body as soon as his breath tickles my skin. I lift my eyes to look at his, with only a soft smile sweeping my face. He walks past me, and I take in his scent, citrus with the perfect amount of warmth. Versace Eros — the same cologne sitting on his bathroom counter when I was choking on his cock.

Kill me now.

Ford emerges from his room and sweeps his arm around Katie's waist before kissing her cheek. "Should we order a car or drive?" He asks.

We agree to get an Uber since we'll drink — even Katie. She giggles when I remind her she told me she was going cold turkey for a month.

"Eleven Park?" The driver confirms as we pile in.

Rhett in the front and Katie, Ford, and I squished in the back. Once we get to the restaurant, we're immediately greeted by the host. Ford handles the reservation as I look up at the ceiling, the whole cathedral of it is lined with paned windows. A large chandelier falls from the center of the main room, and beautiful large potted trees are used as accent plants. The lights cast a soft gold glow throughout, with the only other light source from the city outside pouring down in the restaurant. We follow the host to our table, a four-seater. I follow last in line as Ford and Rhett sit on the same side. Katie sits across from Ford, and I...take the only seat left. Starring directly at Rhett all night will not help my desire, especially when he looks like *that*.

We ask Rhett about his day at work and tell him to give us all the details. Eventually we're greeted by our server, Amanda...or Bethany I forgot her name already — but our drink orders have been put in. In celebration fashion, the boys ordered Johnny Walker Blue. Katie and I are both splitting a bottle of Dom Pérignon.

I know Katie is probably wondering how we can afford all of this, but I truthfully don't have the heart to tell her we just swipe our parent's credit cards without telling them. It makes us seem rotten, but in reality, we only ever wanted the bare minimum from them. When I was eleven, I met a girl at school who told me her parents took her to the movies over the weekend. I remember crying in the bathroom the entire lunch because I had wished my parents would love me enough to do that. Something so easy, inexpensive, and simple…it only required their time — and that was the issue. They never had time for me, for us. Instead, they just threw us their credit cards — thinking that was an acceptable form of love. They haven't told us to stop, and we figure, they are content enough, letting us rack up their bill instead of checking in on us.

Our drinks arrive as we give the menu a final glance. We've already decided to try five appetizers for the table and split four main courses. We want to try everything we possibly can tonight.

"We will have the foie gras, caviar, oysters, roasted bone marrow, and…what was the last one?" I glance over at Ford.

"Tartare." He says to the waiter.

"That's right," I whisper. "Thank you." I say before the waiter walks away. "We're going to be full before dinner." I laugh.

"Remember the time I burned that pizza when we lived in LA," Rhett says, laughing.

"Oh my god, I was literally just thinking about that!" I squeal. "We didn't eat a fucking thing all day and came back to our house. Our parents weren't home, and there was no food besides one *fucking* frozen pizza." I say to Katie before I take a sip of my champagne.

"Yeah, and Rhett fucking burned it to a crisp." Ford laughs loudly, and the whole table erupts with him.

"Okay, but that wasn't as bad as when Rhett ran out of gas at one thirty in the morning when we were all in the middle of the fucking desert in Arizona." He continues to laugh.

"Holy shit, I forgot about that." Rhett chimes in.

"God, I was so scared. I thought we were going to get murdered." I giggle.

"You guys have lived in a lot of places? Huh?" Kate asks.

"Oh shit." Ford lets out a deep chuckle.

"We've been everywhere," Rhett says.

"I told you I wasn't ever in a place long enough to have friends." I hold my champagne glass up to Katie and smirk.

"What was your guys' favorite place?" She asks with a flushed grin.

"Oh, one hundred percent Miami," Rhett says. We all snap our heads quickly, surprised. I would have for sure guessed anywhere in California. "Guys, I was nineteen. It was a great fucking time." He laughs.

"Yeah, yeah, I agree. I liked Cali though," Ford says.

"Me too. I think that would be my pick. But Miami was fun as hell." I say.

"How come California was your twos favorite?" She asks as she points between Ford and me.

"For me, it was the longest we'd ever actually stayed in one place. California felt the most like home, I guess." I say before I finish the rest of my champagne.

"Yep. Same. And surfing was fun." Ford says.

"Did that make it hard to have relationships? You moving around so much?" Katie asks.

"Relationships? Yes. Sex? No." I snort as I pour more champagne into my glass.

My eyes drift to Rhett as I set the bottle back into the bucket with ice, only to notice his gaze is struck on me while he's leaned back slightly in his chair, tracing his finger gently over the rim of his glass. I observe him for a moment. The way he looks at me so intently it's as if I can feel the heat directly on my body.

"Emilia, you had like eighty boyfriends shut up." Ford laughs, breaking the spell Rhett has on me.

"It was not eighty!" I squeal with an open smile as I throw my napkin at him.

Our waiter arrives with the appetizers and another round of drinks for the guys as we scramble to move our glasses, silverware, and napkins to make room for the million things we ordered. Before our waiter leaves, we make sure to order our entrees, but my eyes are stuck on Rhett again. Watching his mouth open slightly while he sips straight whiskey sends some fucked up signal to my brain that causes me to lick my lips. I quickly pull my lower lip in with my teeth, hoping it wasn't noticeable, and shift my focus back to Katie beside me.

"You're going to have to show us around Chicago, Katie. Are you up for that?" I say as I tilt my champagne flute to her.

"I am." She clinks her glass with mine.

We each fill our small plates with different appetizers, tasting and raving about each one. I expressed heavily to Katie that Caviar tastes better with champagne, which happened to be when we finished our first bottle.

I can feel Rhett's eyes burning heat onto my skin. It's like he doesn't give a shit if anyone catches him staring at me. I don't give him the satisfaction of letting him know

I notice, so I focus on Ford and Katie, nodding along with the conversation. I shift myself in my seat, leaning an elbow on the table to expose my neck and décolletage in his direction. I nod again with Ford and Katie and lightly trace the tips of my fingers on my shoulder for what seems like several minutes. I notice Rhett shift in his seat from the corner of my eye, and he clears his throat as I continue to trace near my collarbone and realize now, at this very moment, he's thinking about fucking me again.

And I'll gladly let him.

"So this weekend, Katie...are you free to start our sightseeing?" I giggle.

"Absolutely." She replies.

"Boys?"

"Sounds good to me." Ford says.

"I'm in." Rhett replies.

My pulse remains rapid at just the thought of Rhett still wanting me, I can't seem to slow it down, even with taking tiny sips of Champagne. The heat between my legs is rising just as much as the heat on my cheeks so I excuse myself. Once I'm in the restroom, I stand in front of the large mirror that covers most of the wall, leaning on the counter and observing what might have been Rhett's view at the table. My nipples only slightly protrude through the thin material and champagne color of my dress. The cowl neck hangs low enough to at least tell the size of my breasts, just enough for him to remember what's underneath. I smile at the thought of it, but as soon as that smile sticks, I remember what's actually happening.

What's happening is that I had sex with my brother's best friend behind his back. Not only that, I actually have feelings for this man, this man I've grown up with, that's like a brother — *to me.*

I've got to stop doing this.

I need to move on. It was just sex — *clearly* nothing more and *clearly* never happening again. I should shift all of my focus to Jacob and our date tomorrow. I hope it will be decent enough to help me leave whatever this is between Rhett and me, in the past.

I need all the champagne I can get right now to block out the remembrance of the last twenty-four hours.

I get back to my seat and we indulge in our dinners — sharing and passing plates around so each of us can try everything. This is probably the best meal we've had since coming here.

I stand up out of my seat once the bill is paid, and it was either the quickness of my jolt upwards or polishing off that second bottle of champagne, that made my strap fall off my shoulder. Before I can pull it up myself — Rhett's fingers graze my skin and push it up for me, sending a sting of electricity shooting down my arm. The pit of my stomach flutters once his fingers pull away from my body, and now, I'm feeling less confident I can stay away from Rhett tonight.

Chapter 11

Emilia

Do you guys want to go to Captain Lou's? It's a bar right down the street. You'll love it!" Katie asks excitedly as we exit the restaurant.

"I would love to, but I'm so exhausted, and I have to be at work three hours earlier than you do tomorrow." I groan to her.

"I'm down!" Ford smiles.

"I think I'm with Em. I'm beat and have to be to work about five hours earlier than all you mother fuckers." Rhett laughs.

The pit appears again in the bottom of my stomach, and I'm trying hard to keep my shaky breath quiet. Does Rhett really need to go home? Or does he want to be alone with me? Maybe I'm being too optimistic. He said it himself, we can't do it again.

As soon as we're in front of our door, I realize I don't have my keys on me, so I lean on the trim and watch as Rhett pulls out his key from his pocket to unlock the door. My body sways as I lean, but I'm only trying to keep still. I look at Rhett's side profile, his features are soft, with no clenched jaw, and no burrowed eyebrow lines. His hand holding the key looks large in comparison, and the veins become more noticeable as he twists the door handle. The only thing my mind wants to do is think of that hand around my throat.

He pushes the door open, and I follow him in, accidentally stepping on the heel of his shoe that is in front of me. He falls forward slightly as I trip forward onto him. We laugh as he turns around.

"I'm so sorry." I giggle and hiccup.

"It's okay." He smiles as he grabs my arms to stabilize me.

We walk into the kitchen, and the smile still rests on my face. "Did you have a good dinner?" I ask softly as my eyes flutter through my lashes to look up at him directly.

"It was very fucking good." He says in a low tone.

"I agree." I grin.

"Can you...help me get this?" I ask as I turn around and sweep my curls to the front of my shoulder, directing him to the zipper on my dress.

A brief pause is set between us and we stand in silence before I feel his fingers reach the middle of my back. He pulls lightly on the zipper as it moves down slowly. I keep my hands placed on my breasts to hold up the front of my dress as the straps fall off my shoulders.

"Thank you." I say quietly as I turn around and tilt my chin up to look him in the eyes again.

His gaze remains locked on mine, and my pulse beats so heavily I can *hear* it at least ten times before all my thinking flies out the fucking window, and I let my dress fall to the floor.

His jaw stiffens with no other words between us as I stand in front of him with nothing but a black laced thong. His breath becomes more shallow as I watch his chest cave slightly in each time he inhales. His eyes fall to my breasts as I watch him swallow hard and grip the island countertop behind him so tightly, the whites of his knuckles begin to show.

I don't know what I'm doing. Every part of me wants to not need him, to not crave him this way. Every part of me wants to move on from this man, from this, *thing*, that we're doing. *But I can't*, and the more I try to resist, the harder it becomes.

Without so much as a second thought, I fall to my knees in front of him.

"Emilia." He demands in a gruff voice.

I take a deep breath while my chin is still tilted up at him. He slowly brings his hand to my face, hooking his finger under my chin to brush my bottom lip lightly with his thumb.

"I've been thinking about fucking up your makeup all night." He says as his mouth drops slightly and a sinister grin sweeps across his lips. "Making your mascara run..." He trails off while he applies more pressure to my bottom lip. "Smearing your lipstick..." He says as he sweeps the creamy color off to the side of my mouth.

"One last time." I plead softly with him as my eyes flutter back at his.

I kneel before him, practically begging for him to put himself in my mouth. I can feel my heart start to sink as the silence only grows stronger. My eyes scream at him, pleading for him to take me, because my words can not.

"Get in your room." He sighs hard as his lips press together.

I stand up slowly and grab my dress before I walk to my room. He follows behind, and a small grin sweeps my face, *a grin he can't see.*

I hear my door shut and immediately turn around as I keep my hands behind my back, holding them together near my ass while my breasts are on full display for him. He stands with his back on my door before stepping closer to me and taking off his suit jacket. He tosses it on my bed before he turns around and locks my door, only to look back at me with a stiffened jaw while he unbuttons his dress shirt and yanks the tails of it out of his dress pants. I smirk as I see his bare chest. The memories of his body on mine flood my head as he throws his shirt on my bed, landing directly on his jacket.

"Come here." He demands.

My heart races as I take three steps to him, nearly flush against his body. He grabs my waist with one hand while the other sweeps to my neck and firmly rests behind my ear. His grip tightens as he brings his face closer to mine, holding me there as our lips nearly touch. The only sound either of us make is our heavy breathing into each other's mouths. He takes a moment before he forcefully presses his lips on mine. I part my mouth open to let his tongue dive in and push my tongue into his mouth almost at the same instant. He kisses me with intent, with force, before he turns me slightly to shove me hard against the wall. His face pushes on mine as he continues to dive his tongue into me and his hand slowly moves closer to the front of my neck, as his thumb grazes the tip of my chin. He slightly pulls his lips away from mine as he pants heavily into my mouth before his grip tightens around my throat.

"Fuck." He mutters under a clenched jaw before he pulls my neck forward and slams my head to the wall. Not enough to hurt, but enough to show force.

A sadistic grin forms on my face, and his lips brush against mine when he speaks.

"I can't stop thinking about how pretty you look when you cum." He says before he slams my head against the wall again, only pulling it forward no more than an inch.

I stretch my lips in a smile as he grabs my throat tighter.

"I want to see you cum, Emilia. Do you think you could do that?" He whispers into my mouth. I nod my head *yes* as the corner of my lips stay curled up.

He moves the hand gripping my waist to the front of my thigh as his finger lightly grazes the lace trim of my thong back and forth before he pushes the fabric to the side to trace my slit the same way.

"You're so fucking wet already." He groans softly into my mouth.

I whimper as our lips touch again, and in an instant, he shoves two fingers inside of my entrance. I moan loudly as I feel the force of his fingers bury inside of me, his knuckles pressing right against me as the palm of his hand causes friction with my clit, rubbing on it faster and faster. He curls his fingertips inside of me, pressing on that spot I love.

"Fuck." I whimper as our lips part, and our foreheads press hard together.

His grip on my throat remains tight but not hard enough to block my windpipe. He thrusts his fingers into me, alternating curling his fingers. The sound of my wetness splashing against his hands tightens my pussy, and I moan as I place my hand on his thick cock through his pants. I can feel him already, throbbing hard. He groans as I stroke him back and forth, and I grab the back of his head with my other hand as I press him into me, so he falls to the crook of my neck. He places his open mouth on me, licking and kissing my neck before he bites down. I cry out at the sensation, and he kisses me higher, biting on my chin slightly and running the flat of his tongue on my skin wherever it falls.

"I'm coming." I whimper with my mouth dropped open as my chin quivers.

"Cum, baby." He groans as he continues to force his fingers inside of me.

He thrusts harder as I cry out, going faster as my eyes roll to the back of my head. He pulls his fingers out and rubs his flat hand over my clit, faster and faster. My wetness sprays all over us, casting specks on his dark pants.

"Fuck." He moans as I continue to spray him.

The look on his face as I orgasm causes me to cry out even louder. His mouth is dropped slightly while his eyes look desperate for me, his brows raise, and his breathing intensifies.

My cries eventually become silent as my throat closes with no air, only until I'm finished, and I finally gasp as my body stops convulsing. He covers my mouth with his as his tongue dives back inside me, and I stand there, flimsy from the exertion but still held up by his hand, pinning me to the wall from my throat.

"Get on your fucking knees." He demands in my ear.

Without hesitation, I drop in front of him, the bottoms of my feet now resting against the wall.

He hastily removes his belt and unbuttons his pants, and I look at the wetness I caused on him. Darker flecks stay on his black pants as they drop down to his ankles, and I try to catch my breath during the brief pause. I tilt my chin up to look at him and open my mouth while I stick out my tongue with only a weak smile drawing on my face once I see his cock in front of me — stiff as hell with veins that run down the length.

I need him all the way in the back of my fucking throat.

He grabs his cock and slaps it a couple of times on my tongue before he shoves it in— grabbing the back of my head with one hand. He groans loudly as I take him in my mouth. I lick and suck as far back as I can before he takes matters into his own hands.

He thrusts his hips and fucks my mouth as hard as he can. My gagging doesn't subside and gets louder as I try to keep myself from coughing. He moans at the sound of my gags before he pulls out of my mouth, the saliva drips down my chin and hangs from the tip of his cock to my tongue. I look him in the eyes and see his grin.

"There we go." He breathes as he wipes a tear that's falling down my face. I can feel the clumps of my mascara running with it. He thrusts back into my mouth as I bring both hands to his cock, running it up and down the length while I suck on the tip.

"Oh god." He groans loudly. His palm slaps my face once he pulls out of my mouth again and I smile wide.

I was waiting for that.

He pulls me up by the arms and brings me to the bed, pushing me down before he lifts my legs apart. He grabs his cock and runs the tip up my slit before shoving himself inside of me. We moan at the same time he's in, and he pauses to adjust. Bringing one hand to the underside of my thigh to push on to, the other hand pulls me up in a crunch by the back of my neck. He plunges deep inside of me slowly at first before each thrust turns harder. He pounds into me with force, and I scream. He grunts as he thrusts, and I keep his gaze on me while my mouth stays dropped open.

We breathe into each other for a brief moment, and that's when I hear it.

The front door shut.

I whip my head to the side to listen closely as Rhett plunges into me over and over again. A groan accidentally escapes my mouth, and he instantly lets go of the back of my neck and pushes his hand over my mouth to silence me. I hear Ford's footsteps get closer as Rhett pushes hard to muffle my sounds, only making a sliver of space between his fingers and my nostrils to breathe. I cry out into his hand as he continues to thrust. He grabs my breast with his free hand and pinches my nipple between his fingers, my eyes roll as I moan, and his hot mouth falls to my breast. He takes my nipple between his teeth slightly as he pounds me. He brings his face close to mine, his hand still blocking the space between our lips. Sweat beads drip off his nose and hair onto my skin and sizzle once it hits.

"I'm gonna fucking cum." He moans quietly as he releases his hand from my lips.

I take a big gulp of air as my mouth hangs open before his lips collide with mine. Our tongues roll around together before he stands up straight to the side of the bed and grabs my hips, driving harder into me as I cover my mouth to stop the escaping screams.

"Oh fuck." He whispers as he shakes his head slightly, a look of desperation on his face like he doesn't want to cum yet. He slaps my breast and squeezes while he plunges hard one last time before coming. He groans as quietly as he can while he drains himself — inside of me, *again*.

Fuck.

He collapses on my body. Our hard breathing matches up as we try to calm our heartbeats.

"Emilia..." He murmurs.

I close my mouth and breath through my nose. I don't know why I feel like crying right now. I know what he's about to say. I don't want to hear it.

"We can't — "

"I know," I say flatly, cutting him off.

I slowly turn my head to the side as I bring my hand to my eye and wipe the back against a falling tear. My chest rises and falls heavily as his body still lays on mine. *Glad to see he's at least learned some aftercare etiquette — that'll be great for the next girl.*

I take one last deep sigh and prepare to face the fucking facts. He doesn't want me in this way anymore. It's done. I tried, and still... it won't change anything.

I shift my mindset in a snap — no more crying. I start to sit myself up to give him a hint to do the same. He climbs off of me, and I walk to my bathroom and shut the door. I stand still for a moment. I don't even know what I have to do in here. I just wanted to be away from him. I hear my bedroom door shut quietly, and my body deflates with a heavy sigh. I turn on my shower and wait until it's hot before I step in and let the water run over my body and soak my hair before I sit on the tiled floor and bring my knees to my chest. I lay my left cheek on the top of my knee and close my eyes.

I just want to be loved — and for some fucked up reason...I want to be loved by Rhett.

Chapter 12

Rhett

The last thing on my mind right now is building this stud wall, and I find it hard to focus on the actual work I'm supposed to be doing. I wipe the sweat from my forehead as I hold the ceiling plate in place, giving me just enough time for my eyes to close briefly before I get another flashback.

I wasn't lying when I said all I had thought about was ruining her makeup, and *I did*. But god dammit, that has to be it.

"Adler! Help me snap this line." My coworker says from behind me.

I already forgot his name, but I'm sure I'll remember it when I'm not thinking of Emilia's tanned skin contrasting against that very light, very thin dress that showed her perfect fucking nipples through.

I would have been just fine last night — just getting home and going to bed, but she begged. How was I supposed to say no — to *her*, begging at my feet like that? I can't imagine it makes her feel good, me telling her we can't fuck anymore. It's not that I don't want to. I wish I could explain...but I think telling her the truth will cause more harm than good, and I'm already making her feel worthless, I'm sure of it.

I have to tell her.

I just don't know how.

As soon as I finish framing a wall, my phone buzzes in my jean pocket. For a slight moment, her face flashes in my head, but I know it's not — she wouldn't text me privately like that, Ford's phone is always dead, and he's constantly using mine. He'd kill us both if he ever found out.

I have a second to glance at my phone —

FORD BARDOT: Emilia won't be home later, so what do you want to eat? We could go to that wing place by the fire department.

RHETT: Sounds good.

Where's she going?

FORD BARDOT: Some date.

Said we were on our own for dinner.

Well, great...good for her. Probably with that fucking arrogant prick, but it's fine... that's good. I'm happy for her, then, I guess. Emilia's had plenty of boyfriends before, and I've never allowed myself to get jealous. I sure as fuck can't start now.

Whatever I feel for Em — whatever I have been feeling, needs to end. She knows that too. Not to mention what we're doing to Ford in the process.

He can never find out — plain and simple.

I've got to stop staring at her, though. It's never been a problem before. I don't know why it is now. It's like I can't stop myself like I'm some persistent lion that keeps going to the watering hole just to see what he can eat today.

I make it through a couple of hours of saw cutting before my mind shifts back to her, the sweet sound of her voice when she says my name — the even better sounds she makes when she's squirting.

Shit.

Enough, Rhett.

I've got to reel it in. For fucks sake.

"Do you think I could take my break now?" I ask the site manager, Louis.

He checks the time on his watch and nods his head. I set a piece of plywood down and walk towards a fence as I pull my phone out of my pocket again.

RHETT: Let's get fucked up tonight.

FORD BARDOT: Deal.

I need something, *anything,* to rid my mind of her.

Chapter 13

Emilia

I got home from work today before anyone else.

Thank god.

I haven't spoken to Rhett, and I let Ford know I have a date tonight, so the boys are on their own for food. Of course, I'm desperately hoping Ford lets Rhett know the reason I'm not home — I want to make that fucker jealous, if anything.

I *also* want to look nice for Jacob tonight. He seems like a sweet guy. He's fucking gorgeous, and he has an interest in me. That's a plus. Who knows, Jacob could be my fucking soulmate, and Rhett was just a bump in the road to get here.

I love this new version of me that I created in the last eight hours...thinking like an opportunist. Really mature of myself.

I decide on black ripped jeans and a sweetheart neckline frilled long sleeve for our date. I'm going for *cute girl next door*, not an *awful fucking slut* like I truly am. My hair is tousled with large curls — think, *Victoria Secret Runway*. And my eyes are lined with a wing at the end. The false lashes that I used are called *Sweetheart,* and my lips are a soft pink, only dabbed in the center of my lips to create more fullness than I already have. I step back and glance at myself in the mirror, then slap on whatever kind of smile I can, given the circumstances of my life in the past couple of days. I swipe my phone to check the time and see I have a missed text.

JACOB FROM BAR: I'll be out front in five.

Shit. That was three minutes ago. I grab my purse and put on my wedges as I hop and skip through the kitchen in the foyer. Shutting off the lights and then locking the door behind me as I leave.

I stand in the lobby of my apartment building and glance out the large doors, looking for the car Jacob said he had. *Audi R8, Audi R8,* I don't know what the hell that is, but he said it's dark gray. I squint my eyes to help the glare from the buildings around me when I see a slick car pull up with bright, thin headlights. I hear the engine as it pulls up and see the Audi logo. I walk through the front doors and see Jacob getting out, rounding the car to meet me.

"Hi." I say with a smile as he grins and grabs the lower of my back, bringing me in for a hug.

"You ready?" He smiles as he opens the door for me.

I get in, and while he makes his way back to the driver's side, I look around the car. It smells nice in here, almost like a faint cologne, but not the kind he was wearing when I grasped it from the hug we shared. The main interior is black, while the seats are button stitched in a light gray.

"You look great, Emilia." He says once he puts the car in drive and glances over at me. His hand rests on the shifter while his seat leans slightly back.

"So do you, Jacob." I smile. "Where are we going?" I ask sweetly.

"Are you hungry?" He asks.

"Starved."

"Good. I'm going to take you to a little Italian place. Do you like Italian?"

"I love it. There's not much I won't eat." I giggle.

"I love that." He says as he glances to the right at me. He moves his hand from the shifter to my leg. His touch feels cold from his hands. "How has work been this week?" He asks.

"Pretty good. I'm still learning the ropes."

"When I first met you, you said something awesome happened. What was it?"

"God, I can't believe you remembered that." I chuckle. "Um, well... on my first day, I had to write a freestyle article, like a trial article, the magazine called it. They wanted to figure out where to place me within the company, and long story short, I wrote the article, and it's getting published in next month's issue." I grin widely.

"Jesus, Emilia, that's fucking incredible." He says with wide eyes and an open mouth.

"Thank you."

We pull into a parking garage, and he finds a spot near a door inside. Before I can unbuckle, he's parked and out the door, rounding the front to open mine. I get out and flash him a grin with my lips pressed, thanking him for the chivalry, surprised that's even a fucking thing anymore. We walk into the doors and down a hall, with large elevators on the left and a glass front door on the right. We turn to the left again and continue to walk until we come upon huge french doors with the word *Tavolo* written in beautiful cursive. *Food. Drink. Dessert.* It reads underneath in a smaller font. The red color of the letters almost looks velvet against the frosted glass.

Jacob opens the door for me, and I walk in first, taking note of the darkness inside, with the only light beaming from the yellow glows of the lamps by each table. The bar in the center of the room is grand, and the dark oak wood shines bright, even in the dimness. Every top-shelf liquor you could think of is placed in front of a mirror behind the bar, and waitstaff is dressed in sleek black — I even see one scraping crumbs off of a patron's table before their next course is served. This place is swank. Ford would like it here too.

"This way." Jacob says as he takes my hand and walks through the restaurant, weaving around tables as we work our way to the back.

I've been to a lot of restaurants, and I don't think this is the right way to find a table, especially with the fanciness such as this one. But I follow — willingly trailing behind him as he pushes through the kitchen doors. Staff and chefs smile at us as we push through another set of doors to a different room with few tables, all two-seaters, and all empty. He pulls the chair out from the table for me to sit. I smile with confusion at him, and he just raises an eyebrow.

"For you." He smiles.

I sit, and he takes the seat across from me. A small black lantern with a candle is the only thing between us. I feel a presence to my left and look to see a waitress right besides us.

"Hello Mr. De Luca, can I get you and your guest something to drink." She says stiffly like she's some sort of — professional robot.

"Do you like red wine or white wine?" He asks me.

"Let's do...red?" I say, half in a question, half certain.

"Can we get a bottle of that new Pinot Noir that just came in?" He asks before she nods once, drops the menus at our table, then exits through the set of kitchen doors.

"So..." I trail off, still with a confused smile. "Is this...?" I don't even know what to ask him at this point. He looks my age. I can't imagine he owns this place.

"My dad owns it. He came to Chicago a couple years after me. I guess I talked the place up enough. Since I didn't have much going on, he hired me here. Just to do bookwork and things like that." He says.

"That's...amazing." I say, my confusion leaving my face. The car, the clothes, the fucking looks.

Rich blood.

My least favorite people.

I did everything I could to not be one. Jacob seems different, though, at least — I hope he is.

"So you said you work for a magazine then. What magazine? And what's your actual job title?" He asks as he glances at my chest, pausing for a moment before lifting to my eyes.

"Thirty8. My actual job title is a Columnist but I'm not writing any other pieces just yet." I explain.

"Cool. Is that what your dream job is?"

"Pretty much. Ever since I was, probably ten, I'd say."

"Sweet. Good for you." He says as the waitress returns with our bottle of wine, showing off the label to Jacob before he nods.

She sets it on her rolling table and slices off the gold-sealed label, uncorks it, then pours a very small amount into Jacob's glass before he brings it to his lips and tastes it. He sets it back down and nods and she continues to pour his glass.

I don't give a fuck about all of that. Just pour me the damn wine. I don't need all of the extras, I just need a drink. She finally pours mine and then leaves.

"To getting to know you better." He says as he tips his glass to me.

"Cheers," I smirk as I clink my glass with his.

I swish my wine quickly before sipping. Its pungent taste brushes my lips as I swallow. Pinot coating the entirety of my mouth. I forgot I haven't eaten much today, so I better order something quickly before I end up drunk in front of Mr. Dreamy here.

I take a look over the menu as Jacob makes recommendations on his favorite dishes. Usually, I would hate this kind of behavior — overbearing, know-it-all, type. But he doesn't come across as that, only knowledgeable because it's his family restaurant. I settle on the Bucatini alla Calabrese, the one he highly recommended.

"Where are you originally from?" He asks.

I assume he means before Chicago, but that's always a tough question to answer. I divulge in my childhood somewhat. Mostly about us moving and never being in one spot very long. Less on my father consistently cheating on my mother while simultaneously never spending any time with his children.

"Sounds fucking awesome. No rules. Credit cards. No authority. You're so lucky." He says excitedly.

Only I'm not. I'm actually the complete opposite.

Why is everyone so enticed about the fact that my parents were never around, that they didn't even help a single droplet in raising us? I wasn't able to play sports in school. If I had the chance to, I would have tried every sport, at least once. I had to be homeschooled half of the time because we would leave throughout the middle of the school years. The only reason Ford and I got into *any* schools was because we begged our parents, I mean, that screaming kind of begging where the children are sobbing uncontrollably until they can't breathe and their face turns bright red.

"I used to be really jealous of everyone on the car commercials during Christmas time." I say after I take a sip of wine.

"The what?" He asks.

"The car commercials. Usually, the dad would buy the mom a new car for Christmas. He'd bring it home to his family, where his wife and kids would run out in their matching pajamas and jump up and down in their driveway together. They always looked so happy, like, a true family. Or what I would imagine one looked like. I wasn't envious of the car...it was the matching pajamas for me." I explain softly.

"I could see that. But still, trust me, a lot of kids would have rather had your experience." He chuckles.

I clench my jaw in a smile. It's okay he doesn't understand. Not many people do, I guess.

The waitress comes back to take our order. Jacob asks for two appetizers and orders our dinners. We continue talking about Chicago and some fun things to do in the city. I like him, and I like his company. He seems a little young for me. He's twenty-three but his personality is more of a nineteen-year-old who just saw boobs for the first time. He keeps staring at my chest, and by now, I figure he *actually* thinks he's being slick, even though it's very noticeable. Something about it makes me wish I had a fucking turtleneck on.

Once our appetizers arrive, we switch to talking about our past relationships.

Now — I'm not one to kiss and tell. Truth be told, the amount of sex I've had would make it seem like I'm a fucking prostitute, which I'm not...except that one time a boy named Tommy in Utah paid to see my tits, but that was the *only* exception. But as much sex I had, I was also in very short relationships. Usually — I would have sex with someone, we would date, fall in love, and then I would move. Then the cycle repeated itself in a new state.

I only tell Jacob bits and pieces about my love life history. Moving around a lot helps paint a picture of loneliness and celibacy, so I ride that train as long as I can.

"What are you doing after this?" He asks right before the waitress swings the kitchen doors open with a large tray in her hands. I glance at my phone to check the time.

"I probably should go to bed. I'm supposed to be at work by seven tomorrow morning." I lie.

I don't have to be there until nine, but I just want to go home alone tonight. It's been a rough week and a bed to myself sounds heavenly right now.

"That's too bad. Next time we go out, I'd like to show you around a couple places if that's okay." He says sweetly with a smile.

"I'd like that." I grin, and we begin eating.

The pasta I got is delicious, lightly draped in a red sauce. I grin as I taste it and rave about it to Jacob. He gives me a bite of his chicken, and my eyes roll as I moan. The perfect saltiness of the capers with a refreshing hint of lemon.

This is some good fucking chicken.

The food is incredible, and I make sure to let Jacob know.

"Thank you, Mazi." Jacob says to the waitress as she clears our table. "You ready?" He asks me before he stands.

I nod my head yes, and he throws a hundred-dollar bill on the table before walking to me and grabbing my hand. He leads me out of the restaurant the same way we came in and back to his car in the parking garage.

"I'm really glad you enjoyed the food." He says before he starts his car.

"It was really good, and I'm not just saying that either."

He starts the car and extends his right hand to mine, holding on to me while he drives. He lightly traces his thumb over my finger, and the subtle gesture makes me grin slightly. We arrive in front of my apartment complex, and he puts the car in park.

"Thank you for a really nice night," I say softly.

He leans over to me. "I hope we can do this again soon."

"I would like that a lot," I say as I smile with closed lips before leaning into him and softly placing my lips on his.

I hear his breathing become shaky as he parts his lips for mine, kissing me softly back. He runs his tongue slightly into my mouth, so it only brushes the inside of my top lip. I kiss him one final time before backing away leisurely.

"Goodnight," I say as my pressed grin returns, and I get out of the car, making sure to wave to him before I walk away. I don't even make it to the door before he drives off.

I walk inside and head upstairs. I'm so fucking ready to take these wedges off and, dear god, if I don't unbutton my pants in four seconds, I'm going to burst. The elevator to my floor dings, and I walk at a steady pace. I put my key in and turn it quietly, making sure to handle the doorknob with the same care to not wake anyone. I walk in to see the house dark, but as I enter the open space, I can see the bright cast of the TV glowing in the living room. I squint slightly as my eyes adjust. Rhett is lying on the couch with a blanket, his eyes glued on the TV before he hears my footsteps.

"Shit." He says as I startle him. I giggle loudly, trying to keep quiet.

"I'm sorry," I whisper with a smile. "I thought you would both be sleeping. Goodnight." I say before I turn to the left to go into my room.

"How was your date?" He asks me in a low tone, somewhat quietly.

I turn to face him again.

"It was really nice," I say as I inhale a short breath through my nose. "Good night, Rhett."

I walk to my room and immediately unbutton my pants. On my dresser, I see that familiar brown paper bag. My stomach produces a dull pain as I grab it and take it to my bathroom to wash this terrible pill down with tap water. Just one more reminder of Rhett and I screwing. I sigh before slipping my pants off completely and grabbing an oversized t-shirt from my closet to throw on. After I set my alarm for work, I snuggle into my soft sheets and comforter and rest my head.

I really did enjoy my date with Jacob. I only thought about Rhett a few times. Maybe as I continue to date, I won't think about him at all, and this little — *whatever the fuck this was* will be a thing in the past that most certainly does not affect my future.

At least — this is what I'm telling myself.

Chapter 14

Emilia

"Emilia... Emilia... Em?" Rhett whispers in my face as he nudges my shoulder.

"What?" I groan into my pillow while I bury my face in it.

"Ford and I are going to the gym. Do you want to come?" He asks, still whispering by my bed.

"What time is it?"

"It's seven." He says softly.

"Why are you in my room?"

"I was knocking for five fucking minutes, but you could sleep through a hurricane, so I came in."

I groan loudly as I turn over and throw the covers off of me. My eyes are still closed, but I can feel the breeze of air brush on my stomach. I can tell my shirt is crumpled up right under my breasts, and my entire midsection is exposed, showing the small pink stringed thong I have on.

Not like he hasn't seen worse before.

"When are you guys leaving?" I ask as I open my eyes and look at him.

"If you want to come, we will wait for you to get ready. If you're not coming, we're going to leave right now." He says as he looks down at me.

"Give me five," I murmur as I lift my body to sit up.

Rhett leaves my room and shuts the door as I glance to the left and look out my window to the beautiful morning of Chicago. The buildings are somewhat visible through the light fog casting on the city.

I get up and throw on leggings and a cropped mauve long-sleeve top before I brush my hair out and brush my teeth. I pack my work clothes into a drawstring bag because I know I won't feel like coming back to the apartment to shower before work, so I might as well do it there. I walk to the kitchen and see the boys hovering around the island in their gym gear

"Can someone mix mine?" I ask, pointing to their pre-workout as I walk to grab a banana next to the refrigerator.

"Get it yourself." Ford says with a sharp tongue.

"I'll get it." Rhett says after him, giving Ford a look of disapproval.

Rhett grabs a small shaker cup for me and mixes his pre-workout in it. I eat my banana as Rhett shakes it up before handing it to me.

"Thanks." I say with a mouthful of banana. "You bitches ready or what?"

"We've been waiting on your dumb ass." Ford snaps again.

I laugh. He's not a morning person, but he can go fuck himself right off.

"Have you heard from mom?" He asks as we stand in the elevator.

"Just when I called her the day we got here." I reply.

"That's nice. I'm glad they care for our well-being." He says as the elevator doors open to the gym. "I'll be over here." He points to the free weights.

I walk over to the stair master and shake my cup once more before downing it, then I refill it with water from the fountain beside the machine. I glance briefly at Rhett before I climb on. He sits on a bench and curls a heavy dumbbell — his biceps flex every time he brings the weight to his shoulder. I shut my eyes briefly as I breathe in through my nose, *we can do this*. He's not that good looking... I can convince myself of that— let's just think...*juvenile prick, womanizer, asshole.* There we go.

I put my AirPods in my ears and start my machine. Thirty minutes go by while sweat beads on the skin exposed between my top and leggings. The hair framing my face becomes wet and sticks to my forehead as I continue to climb.

"You good?" Rhett asks as he walks by my machine. He wipes a white towel over his forehead, his shirt is off, and sweat glistens on his chest and arms.

Dear god, help me now.

I issue a thumbs up and a half smile. I'm too winded to speak at the moment. He laughs lightly before moving to another machine, and I press the button on mine to cool down for ten minutes.

"You guys about done? I gotta head back before class." Ford asks as I wipe my face and neck with a towel before discarding it in the basket designated for them.

Rhett is sitting on a bench near me.

"I'm done. I'm gonna shower here and head straight to work." I pant.

"I'm finishing up one last set, then I'll be there." Rhett says as he moves his headphones to the side.

"Sounds good. Em, what's for dinner?" He asks as he grabs his shaker bottle.

"Ah, fuck, I don't know. You guys text me some ideas later." I say as I wave, still trying to catch my breath. "Goodbye." I wave behind me as I head into the locker room.

The showers resemble our apartment ones, dark and sleek on the inside with a long bench, but the glass surrounding these is frosted, unlike ours.

I take my bag out of the locker and pull my clothes out. Once I throw my headphones in, I zip it up and shove the bag back in my locker. The loud metal clinks together as I shut the door, and I don't worry about locking it before I grab a large towel. I look at the row of showers and pick the middle one.

I undress in the shower, peeling the sticky long sleeve off my body with my leggings going next before I wrap the towel around me and open the shower door again, only to throw my clothes on the bench in the middle of the walkway. I start the shower hang my towel up on a hook inside and turn my body, letting the water hit my hair as I run my hands over my long tresses.

"Emilia?" Rhett's voice echoes through the locker room.

What the fuck?

"Yeah?" I call out.

I hear his footsteps as they move closer to my shower, and I see his figure lightly through the frosted glass as he stands still, finally facing my door. A moment of pause happens before I open the door slightly.

"Do you need something?" I ask as I peek my head out through the tiny opening I made. My gaze fastened on his.

"Yeah...actually," he sighs as he brings his hand to his mouth, "No...I mean..." He fumbles his words.

I open the door more and stand up straight. My naked body is completely exposed as he stands in front of me. I cross my arms and lean on my back leg. I don't know what he wants from me. The only thing he's doing is confusing me. It's not fair, and I don't need the fucking headache.

"Emilia..." He says as he slightly licks his lips and pulls his bottom one in with his teeth.

We stand in silence some more, and I take a breath and resume my shower. I grab the shampoo and squirt a nickel size in my palm before rubbing it together and lacing my hair with it.

He takes a seat on the long bench behind him and watches me. I rinse the shampoo out of my hair when I see him slightly adjust himself in his shorts. As I scrub the shampoo out of my hair, I know my breasts are bouncing, and maybe I exaggerate my movements. After all, I want him...he's the one that doesn't want me. I squirt the body wash into my hands and rub on myself, making sure to massage my breasts before I rub my hands down my midriff, then I bring them down between my legs. I see Rhett's eyes on me…following my hands like a lost puppy. I bring them back to my breasts and squeeze them before I tilt my head back into the water. I let the stream run down the front of my body, washing the suds off. I hear the bench creak and my head snaps forward. Rhett takes off his shoes and socks, next — his shorts and boxers, and lastly — his cutoff shirt. I pinch my eyebrows together in confusion.

"I don't want to just watch." He says gruffly as he steps in. His cock, fully erect already.

The water hits his chest as I move back, my gaze still stuck on his. He sweeps his hand to the side of my neck and brings my face to him, he swarms my mouth with his lips, and they collide together like they hadn't touched each other in years. Our tongues dart in each other's mouth, as if we can't get there quick enough. I moan into him and take his cock in my hand. His mouth drops open as he groans at the initial feeling of my hand squeezing him lightly. He bites my bottom lip with force before he nudges me back with his head. My legs walk backward until my heels hit the bench that runs along the width of the shower. I sit while his lips still intertwine with mine. He moves through the water stream and kneels in front of me before his lips fall to my pussy.

I gasp as he sucks on my clit before running his tongue along my slit. I grab the back of his head and push him harder into me so his stubble scrapes me while I rock my hips and grind on his face, half angry with him because I know when this is over, he's going to tell me the same fucking thing — *we can't do this again.* I whimper lightly before I hear a locker shut. Rhett and I immediately perk our heads up as I set the leg he had a hold of down. He quietly stands up as the water runs between us. Another shower starting echos to us, and I stand up to peek my head out slightly. I see a woman getting into the shower and shutting the door.

"You should go," I whisper to him. He clenches his jaw and nods once as his eyes flicker shut. He walks out of the shower and closes the door while I stand under the falling stream. I take a couple of deep breaths only to calm my racing heartbeat.

I want to be with Rhett, I don't give a fuck what Ford has to say about it, and I don't give a fuck that Rhett doesn't do relationships. Why wouldn't he? I'm a fucking catch, and clearly, he can't keep his hands off me. He's already said he doesn't fuck a girl more than once..and here I am, proving that statement wrong. He must have *some* kind of feelings for me, right?

I finish washing my hair before I step out and dry myself off. My thoughts continue to run through my head like a fucking Olympic race. I've just got to keep him coming back and then maybe — eventually — he will want a relationship with me.

Ha.

Rhett...and a fucking relationship.

What a goddamn joke.

Chapter 15

Emilia

I didn't get home from work until nine at night. By then, the boys had already ordered sushi and gone to bed. Thankfully, they had texted me and asked for my order, so now I sit on my bed watching The Housewives, eating my phoenix roll with extra spicy mayo.

I want to text Rhett — I've thought about this morning all day, but god forbid Ford sees it, he'll have my fucking neck. I was trying to edit articles at work but every second I was cursing the mystery woman who just *had* to take a shower while we were in there. I decide to just text the group chat instead and hope they are still awake.

THREE AMIGOS

EMILIA: Just got home.
Thanks for the sushi.

FORD: U owe me

RHETT ADLER: If you don't eat it all, I'll take it to lunch tomorrow

EMILIA: K.

FORD: Don't K us, Emilia. That's rude.

RHETT ADLER: Very.

EMILIA: Goodnight bozos.

FORD: Bitch.

RHETT ADLER: Night.

Close enough.

I finish my sushi with, unfortunately, no extra leftovers for Rhett and scroll through my phone, avoiding the five missed texts from Jacob, then get snuggled into bed. Tomorrow, my mother fucking article comes out, and I'm too damn excited to care about anything else going on. I have my alarm set two hours early. I plan to get to work as soon as possible and get my hands on an issue.

I realize I completely forgot to tell my parents, not sure they would give a shit anyways, but I should at least let one of them know. As I lay my head on my pillow, I reach back over to grab my phone.

> **EMILIA:** The article I wrote for my trial is getting published and will be available tomorrow at stands. Just wanted to let ya know.

COLETTE: Cool.
We are in NY, is it here?

> **EMILIA:** No.

COLETTE: Too bad. Would love to see it.

Well, could have gone worse.

I set my phone back on my nightstand and turn the TV sleep timer on for an hour, turning over and closing my eyes while I listen to the sweet sounds of The Housewives screaming at each other.

"Good morning." I say to the two women behind the front desk in the main lobby as I work my way to the elevators. The smile plastered on my face probably makes me look like an adolescent child who just found out they can have cake for breakfast, but I couldn't care less right now. What doesn't help my excitement any is that Katie is the first person I see when the elevator doors slide open. She stands there, holding the new issue in her hands. My mouth drops open, and my smile widens even more.

"Oh my fucking god." I say in disbelief.

"For you." She says as she hands me the magazine. I hold it in my hands and drag my thumb to feel the texture of the matte-coated cover.

"Can you believe it?" Katie asks as she takes steps with me to our cubicles.

My eyes are still fixated on the cover as I take a seat. My chair spins slightly as I plop down, and I re-adjust myself to face Katie.

"Should I open it?" I ask as I lift my eyes to hers.

She nods excitedly as she bites her bottom lip. I flip open the first page and scan each word, taking notice of the font, the graphics, the photos, and the words. I flip to the next page and do the same until I get to page twenty. I stop and trace my fingers over the title, *Fifteen Places To Have Great Sex Besides The Bedroom — By Emilia Bardot.* Holy shit. I stop and stare in awe.

"Did you find it?" Katie asks excitedly as she bounces her leg and brings her finger to her mouth to bite her nail.

All I can do is sit in disbelief, my jaw still descended as she tries to stretch her head farther to the page.

I read the article word for word as if I wasn't the one who wrote it. I run my finger over each photo and graphic that Katie laid around the page, and I can't help but feel such an overwhelming wave of happiness. I fixate my eyes on her.

"It's perfect." I say as I hand her the magazine to look at.

She takes her finger away from her mouth to grasp the magazine from me, then hunches over with her legs crossed while her foot bounces and shakes. I can't help but giggle at the sight of her being somewhat anxious.

"This is so awesome, Emilia. I'm so happy for you. This has never happened in this magazine before. And the fact they threw this together in here in under a week..." She trails off.

"Are there any more copies I can have?" I ask as I thread my fingers underneath the page once she hands it back.

"There's like forty in the conference room right now. Take as many as you want." She says, and without hesitation, I rip the page. Tearing my article away from the binds of the magazine. Katie's eyes widen.

"Can I borrow one of these?" I ask her as I place my hand on a box of tacks sitting on the edge of her desk.

She nods, and I grab a pink one. I adjust myself in my seat and clear my throat before pinning my article to my cubicle wall.

My first decoration.

"Perfect." I smile. Katie pushes her chair away from her desk to see and grins once she does.

"I love it." She says. "Let's go to dinner. To celebrate. And I want to take you to see a couple things. Are you free tonight?" She asks as she turns her computer on.

"That sounds perfect. What time are you working to tonight? I was supposed to stay until six or, whenever I finish with this." I point to a stack of printed manuscripts I'm reviewing.

"Okay, awesome, I've got a lot I need to get done too. We will go whenever you're ready." She says.

I smile and open the extra-large binder clip that's holding the stack of papers in front of me, and I look at my article pinned on my wall one more time as I take a deep breath.

Cloud fucking nine is where I'm at right now, and I don't see how this day can get any better.

Now, almost six o'clock, and my stack of papers have dwindled down to almost nothing. My eyes hurt from staring at the pages and the vivid red pen that I used throughout them.

"I'm starving." I groan after my stomach growls loudly enough for Katie to hear next door.

"You ready?" She asks with a laugh.

"Fuck it." I say as I throw the papers down. "I'll finish them tomorrow."

I scoot out of my chair and grab my purse before I follow behind Katie as we leave the building and walk.

"First, I want to show you something." She says as she skips ahead of me and walks backward with a wide grin.

I smirk at her, wondering what the hell she's up to. We wait for crosswalks, move with the traffic, and continue to walk until we get to a large silver object.

"I present to you — The Bean." She says with a large grin.

I laugh, unsure of what I'm looking at. A huge, silver, bean-shaped sculpture stands before us. The city reflects off of it as I walk closer.

"Welcome to Millennium Park." She says loudly with her arms stretched out. "The sculpture is called Cloud Gate, I think, but we just call it The Bean."

I walk up to it and tilt my chin up. It's massive, and I feel so small next to it.

"Scooch closer. Let me take a picture." She says, waving at me while holding up her iPhone.

"Wait, I want one with you!" I shout.

Katie looks around and finds a lengthy man in a large black coat. "Excuse me, sir, could you take a photo of us really quickly?" She asks as she extends her phone to him.

He smiles at her and takes her phone before she jogs to stand next to me. She wraps one arm around my waist and throws the other arm up in the air to pose. I glance at her and do the same before I kick my foot up.

"Say cheese." The man says as he steadies the phone.

"Cheese!" We both say as we smile.

"Here you go, I took a couple." The man says as he walks to us.

"Thank you." Katie and I say. She pulls up her photos and flips through the ones he took.

"Oh my god, I love it!" I squeal. I turn around again to take in the sculpture before my stomach growls again.

"Let's go eat." She says as she grabs my hand and starts walking. I follow behind her as we trek for at least twenty more minutes. I take in all of the architecture Chicago has to offer, some buildings even dating back to the eighteen hundreds, Katie tells me. We continue to walk until we get to a long brick building and push through black iron doors.

The restaurant has a funky bohemian atmosphere with dim lighting and eclectic chandeliers, not two the same. The only reason I notice is that the host weaves us in and out of tables, hallways, and rooms to bring us upstairs to an open space with multiple little tables. We get seated at one right next to a large window overlooking the Chicago River. It's a little hard to see now because of the darkness outside, but you can easily tell what it is with the building lights surrounding it.

I glance at my phone. No missed texts, no missed calls — nothing. I set my phone in my purse and hang it over the back of my chair before I raise up the menu.

"Moroccan food huh?" I ask with curiosity as I read the menu.

"I swear to god it's so good. I'm down to split anything you want to try." She grins.

I tilt my menu down slightly to flash her a smile. That was music to my ears. I glimpse at the appetizers, already finding three or four that sound mouthwatering.

Katie tells me her favorites and when the waiter comes by, we order drinks. As soon as they arrive she is quick to toast me, the events of today, and the bean. We cheers, and soon after, our Ceviche, hummus, octopus, and beets arrive. Everything we ordered completely takes over our small round table. At least the drinks we ordered come in tall skinny flutes to save us some table space.

"This is the best food I've ever tasted," I say after I swallow a bite of hummus with garlic naan.

"Mhm." Katie nods with a mouthful.

The waiter comes back, and we settle on two main courses since we nearly ate every bit of appetizer we had.

The rest of our dinner is filled with belly laughs, secrets, and lamb and I swear to her I've never tasted any better food. We stay at least a couple of hours *after* we eat just to talk and drink. Katie said this place is open until two in the morning, so we certainly don't rush. I insist on paying for our dinner since she's the one who took me here, *but,* she repeatedly declines and ultimately, wins the war. We decided to take an Uber back and have them drop us off right in the middle of our apartments. I suggested she come home with me, but since it's already one thirty in the morning and Ford hasn't answered her, we assume the guys are sleeping, and it should be time to call it a night.

"Thank you for tonight. I had so much fun." I say to Katie as I hug her goodbye.

"Me too. Congratulations on your big day. I can't wait to celebrate more this year." She says before we let go. I wave to her as I walk the opposite way to my building.

I only have a block to walk by myself, but I spend the entire time replaying the events of my life since my move to Chicago, including yesterday morning — which shifts my mind to wondering if Rhett might be awake.

And if he is... *can we finish what we started*?

Chapter 16

Emilia

Trying to be quiet as a mouse in pitch-black darkness when you haven't lived in a new place very long is quite challenging. It's even more challenging when you're eight Chipotle Infused Tequilas in.

I mumble to myself as I place my hands in front of me, trying to feel for the walls. As I move out of the foyer, the city lights cascade on the furniture in the living room and kitchen. I lean against the wall to take my shoes off, doing the best I can to keep my balance. I giggle to myself as I lose my footing but quickly recover it.

Unfastening my pants is first on my to-do list once I'm in my room.

A cotton tank top and a pair of my ex-boyfriend's boxer briefs are the first things I pull out of my drawers. I'm too full and too tired to spend any more seconds looking for something to sleep in. I plug my phone into the charger next to my nightstand and only get four steps into my bathroom before my phone buzzes.

RHETT ADLER: Are you awake?

I reply *yes* before retracing my steps back to the bathroom, only this time with a grin on my lips. I place my hands on the counter to steady my breathing when Rhett's body emerges into the bathroom with me. I gasp at the sight of him. I wasn't expecting him to be *in here*.

"I wanted to show you what I got today." He smiles with a low, gruff voice like he'd already been asleep tonight. I turn my body to fully face him as he exposes his hand from behind his back, holding a stack of Thirty8 magazines. My eyes widen, and my smile grows bigger at the sight.

"Oh my god, you really bought six of them."

"I told you I was going to. It was a good article too. Gave me some ideas." He says with a smirk.

My eyes roll upward as I laugh.

"Don't roll your eyes at me." He laughs as he squeezes my jaw lightly with one hand.

"Thank you." I whisper with a smile. My eyes only lift to his as I bite my bottom lip gently.

His chest rises and falls as he takes a deep breath and rubs his thumb over my bottom lip — pulling it slightly down as he clasps my chin and pulls my face into his. My breath becomes unsteady, and we only lock eyes for a moment before it's disrupted by the force of his mouth colliding with mine. The magazines drop from my hands only so I can place them on him. I grab his bare arms and run my hands along each curve of his. I hold his face, then the back of his head — wherever I can touch him while his tongue dips into my mouth and swirls around like he can't taste me enough.

I wrap my arms around his neck and he picks me up and places me on the vanity. The heat of our breaths fills the tiny space between our bodies every time we pull away from each other for air. I whimper as his hand grabs the side of my face again before he pulls away from my mouth and leans his forehead on mine. His mouth is dropped slightly while his hands fall to the hem of my tank, lifting it over my head while I stretch my arms up for him. His hands slide up my body to my breasts as he squeezes them with force before his mouth drops to my nipple, and he looks at me through his eyelashes.

His eyes burn with fire as he flicks and sucks my nipple, squeezing my breast and lifting it so I can join him. I stick my tongue out and flick at my nipple with him, barely making it, but the act alone causes him to groan as our tongues lightly graze against each other. His thumb lazily plays with my other nipple, and I let out a soft groan. I lean my body back on the mirror and grab onto the faucet for more stabilization while he bites at my nipple and tugs softly — the stinging pain only lasts a second before I want it again.

My mouth hangs open as I plead for more. He does it even harder this time before he moves his hand inside my boxer briefs, right in the opening that's normally designed just for men. His finger traces my slit, and he smiles as soon as he touches me, letting me know he can tell how wet I am already. I moan and rock my hips slightly, and he brings his lips to mine again — diving his tongue inside as my mouth parts for him and my legs spread wider.

His finger moves quicker before he stretches my opening, shoving two fingers inside of me. I moan into his mouth at the same time he slightly grunts. He thrusts his fingers inside of me, and any silence from us *not* groaning into one another is filled with my gushing wetness every time he pushes in.

He pulls away from me and my breathing remains rapid as I watch him pull down his shorts and boxers. It's almost slow motion, the way they slide down inch by inch. His deep V line seems never ending, and his cock, *fully erect*, is pinned down by the material until he reaches nearly the middle of his thighs. As soon as his shorts are down, his cock springs up and I watch him as he takes hold of it, staring into my eyes.

"Who's are these?" He asks as he tugs lightly on the cotton briefs, his teeth somewhat gritted.

"Tommy's, I think," I say quietly.

It only takes him a small moment to contemplate whatever decision he's making in his head before he yanks the opening of the boxers with both hands and rips the material right in half. I let out a small gasp as the corners of my mouth curl up and his eyes sparkle with brilliance as he matches my smile.

"Fuck." He mutters as he stares at my pussy and drags his gaze up to my stomach, then to my breasts before it falls right to my eyes.

He leans on me as his hand grabs my throat, and the only reaction I have is to grin while my pussy starts to throb. I want him to choke me tighter, I want him to block my windpipe.

I want...*whatever he wants.*

His lips fall back on mine as he kisses me softly, only grazing his tongue on the tip of my lip before he takes both hands and grabs my hips with force, pulling me to the edge of the counter. Our eyes lock and I buck my hips to rub my wetness on his cock as his hand returns to my throat, this time, *gripping tighter*.

"You're so fucking perfect." He whispers into my lips, his breath — hot as fire.

My mouth curls upward before he releases his hand and bends slightly. His arms wrap around my legs and hold me secure as he tilts my hips up just enough to make me even with his mouth.

The moment his soft lips touch my clit, a shockwave runs through my body like I've just been electrocuted. He's *gentle* — sucking and running his tongue up and down my slit, only circling my clit lightly.

A loud cry moves past my lips, one I wasn't even prepared for, and neither was he. His eyes dart to mine and his hand comes full throttle at my face, smashing over my mouth to keep me hushed.

"You have to be quiet." He demands before releasing his hand from my mouth and wrapping it around my leg again.

He buries his face between my legs, roughly moving his stubble over my pussy as his tongue glides up and down my slit — tilting my hips higher so he can flatten his tongue and lick from my ass to my entrance.

He keeps his blue eyes locked on mine as I watch him devour me from this angle. It's fucking euphoric to see the wideness of his tongue split me in half and curl once he reaches the top — to see my wetness pooling in the center of his tongue is almost enough for me to orgasm in itself.

I throw my own hands over my mouth to quiet my whimpers as I grind my hips slightly to push him harder into me. The only thing I can do is grip his head —*failing to get any hair between my fingers because it's too short* — and muffle the loudest scream I *can't* yell as I cum on his face.

I see the ends of his lips curl upward in his dimple grin as he keeps working his tongue tirelessly on me. My legs still shake as I look at our reflection in the shower glass. Every muscle of his back is flexed tight and his biceps the same as they trap my legs in place.

It's such a pretty fucking picture.

His head between my thighs.

My legs stop shaking long enough for him to know I'm finished and, without hesitation, he slaps my pussy with his hand and dives in once more with his mouth, just to suck whatever other piece of my soul he can.

He groans as he tastes me, and I drop my hand from my mouth once he stands up. Catching my breath seems impossible when I need this much air, but I do my best before he grabs my legs and pushes them to each side in as far of a split as I can go.

His eyes flutter back to mine and he takes his cock in his hand, pressing his body on mine as he slaps my pussy with it.

"Fuck." He draws out in a groan as he thrusts into me.

"You feel so fucking good on my cock." He groans with a heavy breath, and his jaw tenses while his eyes fall between us. He watches himself thrust into me over and over again and the sight of it sends even more heat to my core. I moan, and his gaze jolts quickly to mine as I tighten my pussy around his cock.

"Oh fuck, you feel so good." He whimpers as his head falls back slightly.

I moan softly as my head tilts back. His cock fills me completely, and I can't hold in the tension anymore. My heart beats faster in my chest while my eyes burrow. I fasten my gaze back to him, *pleading him* to make me cum.

He grips the back of my neck and brings my upper body closer to his. I tighten around him once more, and he sighs with a smile as his head shakes back and forth. I know he can feel me grip him and another wave of flutters runs over my body, almost as chilled as ice.

"Cum, baby." He whispers into my mouth before his lips push against mine.

I can't close my lips on his — my mouth still hangs open trying to grasp any air I can. Every bit of me wants to cry out at the top of my lungs, I'm so close to coming, and I want it to make a fucking mess on him. The slapping sound of his body against mine fills the room almost as equally as the gushing sound of my pussy and I can't bare it any longer.

Our eye contact is locked and as I look at him, I can't help but see the helplessness sweep across his features, like he never wants this to end, like — he can't stand the thought of not being inside of me, like — *he loves me*.

"What the fuck is going on!" Ford screams at the top of his lungs as he enters the bathroom.

Rhett quickly pulls out of me, and covers himself with his hands.

I gasp at the sight of Ford, and my body seizes after my arms cover my breasts.

"Are you fucking kidding me?" Ford shouts.

I can't speak. The air is trapped in my lungs, and I can neither exhale nor inhale.

"Ford. Listen!" Rhett stammers as he tries to quickly pull his shorts on.

Ford scoffs in utter disgust as he turns around and walks out of my bathroom. Rhett glances at me in horror before he takes off after him.

I hear them yelling as they move to the living room, and I hop off my counter to find my clothes. Their bedroom door slams, and I hear their voices muffled, still raised at each other. I quickly run to my closet, grabbing the largest shirt I can find to cover my body and dart out of my bedroom to the other side of their door.

"How fucking long has this been going on?" Ford screams.

"This was it. That's all." Rhett lies.

"Come on man. You can fuck anyone. Why the *fuck* did it have to be my sister?" Ford pleads.

"I don't know. I'm sorry. It doesn't mean anything. I fucked up." Rhett says.

My heart drops to the pit of my stomach. I press my ear further on the door.

"Don't fucking do it again Rhett." Ford demands. "I swear to fucking god. Don't. Do it. Again."

"I won't. It was a mistake, Ford. I'm telling you...I fucked up." Rhett begs.

I swallow dryly as my breath becomes shaky. I hear footsteps nearing me from the other side, and I bolt back to my bedroom. I try to silence my breathing inside of my room — my door isn't fully closed but I stand in the shadows of it. Ford violently pushes my door open until we're face to face. I see Rhett further behind him in the kitchen.

"Are you out of your fucking mind?" Ford yells at me.

I stare at him, with not a word to say.

"What were you thinking?!" He screams at my silence.

"I wasn't." I mutter with a shaky breath.

"Clearly." He scoffs. "You know who this is, right?" He says as he points at Rhett. "You know he fucks anything that walks, right?" He snarks. "What the fuck are you doing, Emilia?!" He shouts.

"I don't know." I whisper, trying to hold back the tears that want to push through like a breach in a dam.

"He doesn't want you, Emilia." He scorns. His words hit my chest like a dull knife trying to pierce through. "You want marriage? And happy endings? And rainbows and fucking buteries, Emilia? Well, you're not going to get that from him." He demands.

"Rhett," he says as he turns his body slightly towards the doorway. "Do you want to be with my sister?" He asks as his eyes meet Rhett's.

Rhett looks at me, and I see his adams apple move slowly as he swallows.

"No." He says with an emotionless expression.

Ford looks at me with the most hideous *I told you so* face.

"There ya go." He says as his arms flail up and slam on the sides of his body. "And congratu-fucking-lations, by the way." He scoffs before leaving my bedroom and slamming the door behind him.

The sound of my door crashing against the trim is enough to break the barrier, and the tears fall out of my eyes like heavy rain in Seattle. I find it hard to keep my sobs quiet enough to go unnoticed by anyone else in the home, so I throw my hand over my mouth. My closed eyes pinch tightly together and I can feel my face get red as my sobs turn into screams in my hand.

He was right.

Rhett was completely right.

Sex alters feelings, messes with emotions. I didn't realize how much I wanted him until he was standing in front of me, denying he wanted me back.

Chapter 17

Emilia

I've learned I can't fake a smile with my emotions running rampant like this, especially at work. Katie isn't here today, so I don't really give a fuck anyways. I've tried to start my new article to present for next month's issue, but I only get a paragraph in before I erase the whole thing and start again.

My heart physically hurts. I don't know what I expected from Rhett. People like that don't change. They are set in their ways. He's offed marriage since he was fourteen-years-old, and for someone who never wants any kids, he sure is lenient when it comes to pulling out. The man is a walking red flag, but for some reason, it looked orange to me.

I don't fuck girls more than once, Emilia. Too many feelings involved.

But he did — and he was right — too many feelings.

"Emilia, we got some samples from a tea company. Robin would like you to try them for a week and mention it in an article. They have over five hundred thousand followers on Instagram. It could be great for the magazine." Kathy says to me as she leans on the end of my cubicle wall.

"Okay. Great. I would love to." I clench my teeth while trying a different approach to a counterfeit smile.

"Perfect. Here you go! Let me know what you think."

I open the cardboard box and peek inside. Tea bags with white and pink designs are organized by morning, afternoon, and night. I'm not sure how well I can write about this...I fucking hate tea.

My phone buzzes on my desk, and I only glance at it for a millisecond before my stomach drops.

COLETTE: Hello Emilia.
Your father and I will be in Chicago
this evening. We're getting on a flight now.
Dinner at T'Satos tonight at 7. Tell Ford.
We will meet at your place before. Xoxo

Jesus *fucking* christ. Could this day possibly get any worse? I wasn't planning on speaking to Ford today, or ever, but now, I have no choice. I reluctantly type in his name and send him a message.

EMILIA: Mom and dad are flying in.
Dinner at T'Satos at 7 she said.
Stopping by the apartment first.

FORD: Are you fucking kidding me?

No, Ford, I am not. Although I wish on every fucking shooting star and lucky penny that I was. I don't know what he will do about Rhett being there, and I'm trying my hardest *not* to care.

On the walk home, I search the restaurant webpage and look for any indication of dress code or atmosphere. God forbid I under dress for dinner with Colette and William. *He'll* have my head before *she* does. I'm only in my apartment for two minutes before deciding what to wear takes precedence over picking up takeout boxes and folding blankets.

I pull out the two plainest black dresses that Colette has bought me and decide from there. The look we're going for tonight is — *funeral*. I hold up the long Versace one

—straight neckline, thin straps, high slit, and just the right amount of side boob.

A Whore's Funeral is what it's changed too.

I hear the front door shut but ignore it. I don't care to see either of them right now.

I get to work on my hair and makeup. Dark red lipstick and a heavy winged liner are what I settle on. My hair is in voluminous waves, and I'm surprised it only took me forty-five minutes to come together completely. I finish strapping my heels on and open my bedroom door. I see the mess still isn't cleaned, so I head right to the kitchen island and throw the styrofoam boxes and plastic bags away while trying to keep my long hair out of the trash as I bend to throw it in.

I hear the front door open and then shut — knowing there's a one hundred percent chance it's a man I don't want to see.

I just don't know which one.

Rhett walks into the kitchen, his eyes darting to me in the corner by the trash can. My heart flutters, but not in a *cozy-love* type. It's more of a — *shielding itself from this man* feeling. He stands still only for a moment to look at me before he walks right past into Ford's bedroom and shuts the door. I breathe a winded breath through my nose and walk into the living room to roll up my blankets and shove them in a woven basket that sits in a nook near the TV. My phone buzzes from the kitchen counter, and I stop what I'm doing to grab it.

COLETTE: Should be arriving in
ten minutes. See you soon.

Every bit of my aching soul was praying for a flight cancelation or a delay at least.

"They will be here in ten." I say as I knock on Ford's bedroom door. I hear a groan come from the other side.

"Can you help me tie this?" Ford says after he swings his bedroom door open. He holds the end of his black tie out in my direction as it's wrapped around his neck. I look at him, confused, before my hands adjust it, making one side twice as long before I wrap it around and tuck it. I make sure it's straight before I tighten it to his neck and fix his collar.

"Thank you." He says as my hands fall back to my sides.

I turn back to the living room to finish fluffing pillows in what little time I have left before my sanity flies out of this forty-five-story building.

Ford and Rhett both emerge from the bedroom in suits with ties. I try not to linger when looking at Rhett. I'm so incredibly pissed off at him, and I know I'll never be able to look at him the same, not like I could **P.F.E**...that's *pre-fucking era*.

"We're just going to say Rhett was in town today. That's why he's coming with." Ford says with an unstable pitch to his voice.

I nod. The less I speak to either of them, the better.

A knock comes from our front door, and all three gazes shift directly to it. We don't move until I straighten myself up and run my hands flat along my dress, pressing it out to perfection. I walk through the kitchen past them and into the foyer before pausing at the door. I stand behind it as another knock comes, and I take a deep breath, only trying to collect myself before I open it.

"Hi, guys." I say as I slap on the teeth-clenched fake smile I used at work today.

"Oh, Emilia, you look fabulous." Colette says as she leans in for a hug.

"Emilia." My father says as he nods once with a thin smile.

I open the door further for them to come in.

"Ford!" My mother shouts as she enters the open space. My father follows right behind her.

I watch as she hugs him, and my father shakes his hand. They are pleased that Rhett's joining and talk about how they saw his parents last week. My mind tries to block out what it can. All my life, I've felt like I disassociated every time my parents would speak. I did it on purpose when I was younger, and now, it seems like it happens automatically.

"Shall we get going?" I hear Colette say as my vision hones in again.

"Mhm." I nod with my lips closed tightly, and we make our way down to the lobby and out of the front doors into two black SUVs parked in front.

One for us kids and the other for my parents. They plan to return to the hotel after dinner but assured us our driver is bringing us back to our apartment.

Rhett, Ford, and I pile into the back of the second SUV, me, unfortunately, stuck in the middle since I'm the *smallest* they said. My thighs touch both Rhett and Ford on each side — Rhett having the thigh completely exposed by the slit in my dress. My heart pounds at the closeness of us both, especially since I can smell the cologne on him and how he shifts himself in his seat and adjusts his pants — I can't help but think about his thick...

"Just to let you know, I'm getting black out fucking drunk tonight." Ford states, suddenly jumping me out of my thoughts.

"Me...too." I nod slowly as the words fall out of my mouth.

Rhett flashes a half smile that I can only see out of the corner of my eye. His fingers tap his knee lightly, and I realize with my hand resting on my leg, our fingers could almost touch. I suck in a rush of air and blow out the loudest exhale, anything to calm my nerves. It won't faze Ford. He knows my anxiety peaks around our parents. I've never been prescribed anything for it before and don't intend to. I would, one hundred percent, without a doubt, either sell the drugs or take them with alcohol on a night out. I'm not to be trusted after a small stint with Xanax in my teen years.

We pull up to the restaurant and rush out of the vehicle. I move slower getting out since the slit on my dress exceeds nearly the top of my thigh, a part of me hopes Rhett has a nice view of my bare back with only a couple of thin straps in the way, but my thought is quickly washed out from Colette's shrill voice to the drivers. I tuck a strand of curls behind my ear as I move closer to my parents, waiting for their lead to enter the restaurant.

"Reservations under Bardot, the T is silent." My father says to the host.

"Right this way, Mr. Bardot." She says with a smirk as she leads us to our table. I know my mother is silently dying inside. The host seems to be in her early twenties, thin with long blonde hair, one hundred percent my dad's type, and that little smile she flashed him was enough for him to try to pick her up on the way out.

I haven't felt sorry for my mother since I was nine, and I won't start now. She chooses to be with him despite his many indiscretions.

We take our seats, and being the last in line, unfortunately, gives me the last available seat — which just so happens to be right across from Rhett.

"Emilia, how is work going?" Colette asks me right as the waiter approaches to get our drink order.

"It's good." I snap to her quickly. "I'll take an Old Fashioned please." I say to the waiter.

"Emilia, that's not a proper drink for a woman." William mutters under his breath.

Go fuck yourself, dad.

"I'll have the same." Ford says immediately after me.

"Same for me." Rhett says after him.

I lick my bottom lip before pulling it between my teeth to stop any volatile words that might want to escape in my father's direction while they order their drinks.

"Emilia, don't you think champagne or white wine might be better suited?" My father says after the waiter leaves.

"No, dad, I do not." I gripe at him.

"So, Dad, uh...how long will you guys be in New York?" Ford asks, trying to direct William's attention off of me.

I take a slight breath, somewhat relieved in my feelings. I may loathe my brother right now, and I'm sure he feels the same — but it's nice to know he's still willing to stick up for me.

"We are planning to stay for the rest of the year. It's actually quite nice in the city, and we're trying to expand throughout the East Coast." He replies to Ford.

Thankfully, Ford keeps his conversation going until our drinks arrive. The waiter hands me my drink first, and right as I go to grab it, my eyes accidentally shift directly to Rhett, only to catch him staring back at me. I quickly glance back at my drink before I take a large sip. My nose crinkles as I swallow, but I make no other facial expressions.

"I'll take another," I whisper to the waiter before he walks away. I don't know how slow their service is, but I don't intend to waste any time without a drink in my hand.

"So, Rhett, have you found yourself a girlfriend yet? I'm surprised you boys aren't settled down by now." Colette asks.

Ford clears his throat slightly and my skin warms.

"No, Ma'am, not yet." Rhett smiles.

I try not to look at him. Instead, I try to fish out the Luxardo cherry in my drink with my fingers.

I know.

Real lady-like.

I finally grasp the little dark red bastard and bring it to my lips, only to tilt my eyes slightly because I felt Rhett's gaze on me. I look him in the eyes as I part my mouth slightly and place the cherry on my tongue before I eat it.

The waiter returns to take our order, and I haven't even bothered to look at the menu.

"I'll have whatever you're having." I say to Colette next to me. "I need some air." I announce to the table before I stand up out of my seat and walk to the front door.

My chest feels too tight in this compressed dress to breathe normally. My stomach churns and flips, and I swear I'm on pins and needles every second I'm around my parents. As soon as I push the doors open, the brisk air hits my lungs, and I suck in as much oxygen as I can before letting it all out. I place my hands on my hips and pace slightly. I see a man smoking a cigarette to the right of the doors and take that as an opening to see if I can't calm my nerves this way.

"Do you possibly have one you can spare?" I ask the man as I slowly walk up to him.

His eyes draw down the length of my body as he assesses me. My arms are wrapped around my midriff, and I'm sure the goosebumps are clearly visible on my arms. He reaches into his coat pocket slowly, pulls out a small white and green pack of Marlboro Menthol's, and takes one out for me. He smiles slyly as I take it from him and put it in my mouth. He digs in his pocket and pulls out a lighter before flicking it. The fire burns on the end of my cigarette, and I'm quickly reminded why I don't smoke.

"Thank you." I grin as I walk to the other side of the front doors and lean on the brick building.

I inhale another puff, and my lungs fill with menthol instead of fresh air, but I couldn't care less. Already my anxiety is put at ease as I watch the traffic on the road and look at the tall buildings inside of this city. I take another puff and lean my head back. One arm still remains hugging my midriff, and the other is by my side, holding the cancer stick by my leg. I try to relax my breathing by blowing out with puckered lips, only to have my relaxation come to a screaming halt.

"You know, I heard these things are really bad for you." Rhett says as he leans on the building next to me before taking the cigarette out of my fingers and bringing it to his lips to take a drag. "Where did you get this anyways?" He says after he blows out smoke, his lips curled in a smile as he hands it back to me.

"From a generous man." I say, taking another puff.

"Your second drink is sitting at the table." He says before he pulls it again out of my grasp.

I sigh and tilt my chin to meet his eyes while biting the inside of my cheek.

He takes another hit before he flicks it on the ground and steps on it. "I told them I was going to the restroom. You better get back in there, so it's not obvious." He says.

I suck in my bottom lip and nod, walking past him, back through the front doors.

"Sorry, I didn't feel well for a second." I say as I sit back in my seat. I'm sure the smell of smoke coats the entirety of my skin, but I don't give one singular fuck.

"That's alright darling. I got you a Niçoise salad." She says with a pressed smile.

Only my mother would visit a fine dining restaurant and order a fucking salad.

"I got a Rack of Lamb too, Em — you can have some of mine if you want." Ford says with a soft smile.

I want to hate him so fucking badly. Why does he make it so hard? I issue a small grin to Ford, I'm thankful, but he's still on my shit list right now.

I finish my first drink and immediately bring my second to my lips.

"Emilia," My mother whispers from the side of her mouth to me. "Is everything alright?"

I set my glass down and lick my lips of bourbon. "Yep." I say as my lips smack.

Rhett returns to the table, and my eyes do everything they can to focus on William and Ford talking. Eventually, my mother asks me a few more questions about my work, like she's actually interested.

Before our dinner arrives, we order another drink. The night continues as I barely speak to William and only occasionally look at Rhett. On my fifth Old Fashioned, I need to set my elbow on the table to support my head — I'm extremely exhausted.

Ford and I offer to pay for dinner this evening, but we both know they would never allow that. Eventually, we stand up to leave the restaurant and say goodbye in front of the black SUVs. I have to lean on ours since my balance is a little off.

Ford lends me his hand to get into the truck, and I slide into the middle seat with no elegance or grace in sight. The slit in my dress has become too dangerous for how drunk I am, and now the left side of what little fabric there was is folded up underneath my ass. I groan as I try to shift it.

The leather seat is too cold for my bare skin. I eventually give up as Rhett is on my left, and Ford is on my right — two men that make it crammed in the middle. I lean back on the headrest, and my eyes slightly flutter shut. When my head dips to the left, my eyes spring open. I tilt my head back again, in the center of the seat, and my eyes drift shut again, but this time…I don't open them when my head falls again.

Chapter 18

Emilia

"Emilia." Ford whispers as he shakes my arm. "Emilia, you have to get up." He says a little louder. "You're going to be late for work."

My eyes shoot open as I gasp quickly. I sit up in my bed and throw the covers off of me only to notice I'm in sweat pants. I pull the threads of my oversized t-shirt before I look at Ford, confused.

"We had to carry you up, and — we changed you, well, It was mostly Rhett because..." He trails off, not wanting to admit that his best friend has seen me *more* than naked before. "But don't get any ideas, Emilia. He's not a good guy. Not for you."

It is way too early, and I'm too violently hungover for this conversation.

"We're going out tonight and...I'm going to get him to bring a girl back. You need to see he doesn't want a relationship. He doesn't want marriage...not like you do. I just don't want you getting hurt, Em, and he's my best friend. I don't want to risk losing —" He stops as I bring my finger to his lips.

"I need Tylenol," I whisper as my eyes close.

"Let's just...put this behind us." He says as he holds up two white pills and a half glass of water.

It's not his job to protect me, although I think he takes that role much more seriously than he should. He acts like I'm incapable of handling my own feelings.

I feel I do adequately well, thank you very much.

I take the pills and glass from his hand and down them with one swallow. I don't have time to fuck around, I've got to get moving, or I'll be late. I scramble out of bed while Ford leaves my bedroom and shuts the door on his way out. This is now the second time he's gotten into my room unannounced.

Note to self — lock my bedroom door more often.

"Emilia!" Katie says joyfully as I walk to my desk.

I flash her the best smile I can give with my eyes hidden behind my large square sunglasses.

"Long night?" She asks with a questionable smile crossed on her face. I tilt my eyes over the sunglass rims to see her fully before I notice Kathy walking behind her.

"Hey Kathy, are we allowed mental health days?" I ask as I tip the sunglasses to the tip of my nose. She grins at me cautiously while eyeing me up and down.

"Go ahead, Emilia." She smiles with pressed lips.

Whether it's my unkempt hair or the oversized hoodie filling out my trench coat that wins my case for me, I don't care. *I'm thankful for it.*

"Katie?" I look at her, still with my sunglasses on the tip of my nose.

"Can I —" Katie starts to say before Kathy's smile returns, and she nods yes.

Katie giddily squeals and stands up with me. She takes my arm in hers, and we walk to the elevators. "Let's get you some coffee." She says while she rubs my arm.

I let her guide the way as I have no fucking clue what breakfast places are good here or not. It only takes us five minutes from when we are out of our building to when we are inside another, and for that, I'm grateful for. Chicago weather is no joke nearing the fall.

We sit at a table near a large window, and I take my coat off before I look at the menu, still with my sunglasses in place.

"Their latte's are really good here." Katie suggests.

I find the section on the menu with every coffee they have and browse quickly as our waiter approaches.

"Good morning ladies." The gentleman says with a wide smile and cheerful eyes. "Can I start you off with any coffees, mimosas, waters…"

"I'll take a vanilla bean latte." Katie says.

"Same for me please." I say as I set my menu down.

The waiter nods with pressed lips and walks away to get them.

"Alright — spill it." Katie says as she folds her hands on the table.

"Ha." I say as I cross my arms over my chest. "Where do I start?"

I lean my elbows on the table and slowly take off my sunglasses. My eyes are sensitive to the light, so it takes a minute of squinting to adjust, and I exhale loudly before I divulge.

"Well…Rhett and I had sex multiple times. It started the day after we all went to the club… The last time, a couple of days ago, Ford walked in on us. We all argued. Rhett lied and said it only happened once. Ford asked him in front of me if he had feelings for me, and he said no, straight to my face. Then, my awful fucking parents showed up in town yesterday, *unannounced, I might add*, and insisted we go to dinner. I drank my misery away and had to be carried to the apartment by the boys *before* they changed me into pajamas. Well, not they, just Rhett. So that mother fucker got to see me naked for one last time. And the whole fucking thing is so stupid because Rhett said he would never fuck a girl more than once, and he did...he did it, Katie. He said there are too many feelings involved when you fuck someone more than once, and he's right. I agree because I can't stop thinking about him or the fucking cock he has on him." I get out in a winded breath before I notice the waiter standing at our table with our lattes in each hand.

"Pardon my reach." He says as he places my coffee in front of me.

I toss him a half-crooked grin and look at Katie. Her mouth hangs open while her eyes widen.

"I'll give you ladies a moment to look at the menu." He says before he leaves.

Katie stares at me in shock — or horror, I can't quite tell.

"I thought something was going on with you two." She says as her mouth turns to a sinister smile, and she nods her head slightly.

"Huh?" I ask as my head tilts to the side, and the corner of my top lip pulls up.

"Shit, Emilia...the way he looks at you, I could only *hope* my man looks at me like that one day." She says as she sips her coffee.

"What do you mean?"

"Well, when I first met the guys at the club, I thought you might have already been screwing the way he couldn't take his eyes off you. Then, dinner — the same thing. Whenever he looks at you, his eyes turn warm, not so harsh like I'm assuming is normal for him. You're funny, Emilia, but he laughs at *everything* you say. And his smile is vastly different when he's looking at you and when he's not." She says.

"How so?" I ask.

"When he's looking at you, dimples show on his cheeks. When he's not, they don't. I mean, I've only seen it twice, but it's enough for me to notice a difference. What I'm really surprised about is that you're telling me you just *now* started fucking."

I sip my latte, completely stunned. All of what she said doesn't make me feel any better. If anything...I'm even more confused. My stomach flutters at the thought of him looking at me a certain way, but not for very long as we are interrupted by the waiter.

"Did you ladies have a moment to decide?" He asks as he approaches us.

This man has the worst timing.

"Do you want me to order a couple of my favorites?" Katie asks. I smile and nod vigorously. She knows the way to my heart.

"Can we order avocado toast, sub smoked salmon, and let's get the Nutella crepes, too, please." She says effortlessly.

He nods before he's gone again, and my stomach swirls, this time with the looming thought of Ford's words this morning.

"Ford told me he and Rhett were going out tonight and that I'll see Rhett bring another girl home." I say with an exasperated sigh.

"He said that?" She asks.

"Well, close enough. He wants me to remember what kind of guy Rhett is, so I don't...catch feelings, I guess." I say as I tuck my hand in my sweatshirt sleeve and bring it to my chin to rest my head on. "Too late," I mutter.

"That's shitty." She says as she extends her arm across the table and gently rubs the top of my hand. "I thought that date with Jacob went well?" She asks, trying to change the subject.

"Yeah, it did…he's nice and wants to see me again. I just, I don't know. He's to…entitled for me, I think." I say as I take another sip of my latte. "I don't think I could see him as the father of my kids."

"Do you look at everyone that you date like that?"

"Yes. I mean, having a family is something I've always wanted. I want to have as many kids as possible and be totally present in their lives. I don't care. I would quit my dream job to raise children. It's that important to me."

"Because you didn't have that growing up?"

"I guess…" I shrug my shoulders. "And…I don't know…I don't even know why I would have any sort of feelings for Rhett at all. The man doesn't even want to be married… *but I do*. I want to be married, Katie. I want the whole damn house, with the white picket fence wrapped around my yard. I want to spend the rest of my life with one man, and have kids that run around making a mess everywhere. I want it Katie, and I want all of it with—" I stop, as my eyes drop to my hands that are resting on the table. "Please…don't tell Ford any of this." I say after some pause.

"My lips are sealed." She says as she mimics zipping her mouth shut and throwing away the key. "Well…now that we have the day off work, wanna go bowling?"

"Bowling?" I snort.

"Yeah — bowling. Do you like it?"

"I've never really...bowled before." I stammer.

"Jesus Christ, Emilia, you haven't lived. Oh! Also, I forgot to give this to you before we left the office." She says as she grabs her purse from the seat beside her and pulls out a photo. She hands it to me, and I merely glance at it before my cheeks turn warm, and a smile stretches on my features.

"I love it." I say softly as I rub my thumb over the shiny photo of Katie and me at the bean.

"I thought you might want to hang it up...you know, decorate your cube a little more." She says with gleaming eyes.

"Thank you." I grin as I hold the photo to my chest before I stick it in my purse.

It's only moments after that, the waiter arrives with our food, and I eat like I haven't eaten in days. My hangover only slightly subsides after I get a Bloody Mary before we leave, *hair of the dog* I guess.

As we come up to the building, the only indication of what's inside is a lit-up sign that says BOWL in red. I've only seen people bowl in videos and movies. It just wasn't something us as kids ever did, and our parents sure as fuck would never have taken us.

We walk up to the counter, where we are instructed to tell them our shoe size. Soon enough, they plop down a pair of sevens for me in the most hideous clown shoes I've ever seen.

"Do we have to wear these?" I ask as I hold them up with one hand by the heels.

"Yes." She laughs. *I'm failing to see the joke here.*

She tells me to pick out a ball, but I'm not sure what to choose because they are all heavy as shit.

"You want some weight on it to knock the pins down." She explains.

I choose a shiny purple one, which looks almost like how I would imagine our galaxy does. I waddle it over to where Katie sets her ball down before I sit on the long seat and remove my shoes.

"Do other people wear these shoes?" I ask as I put the first clown shoe on.

"Yes, Emilia." She continues to laugh. "Have you seriously never been bowling?"

"Never." I say as I tie the laces.

A server comes by our section to hand us menus. We've already eaten — but more importantly, they do serve alcohol here.

"Wanna get shit-faced?" I ask as I glance at the menu.

Katie looks at me with confusion as it's only eleven in the morning.

"The guys are going out tonight. I'd like to be asleep by seven." I add.

Katie nods. "Yep. Let's get fucked up."

And so we do.

Chapter 19

Emilia

"All's I'm — All's I'm trying to say is, you're the best, and anyone would be lucky to have you." Katie slurs.

We keep our arms around each other's necks as we sway back and forth on the sidewalk until we get to my apartment.

I laugh and snort while I lean on the marbled stone by the front doors, only to stabilize myself.

Katie and I had buckets filled with three different liquors that came with umbrellas and cherries, and that was all we needed to keep us happy. Also, I learned I'm not terrible at bowling…well, after they added the bumpers to the sides. Katie and I couldn't keep our balls straight enough to get any points in the first game. By the second, we were pros, probably because we were on our second bucket by then too.

"What time is it?" Katie mumbles.

"A little after three." The words tumble out of my mouth slowly. "Do you want to watch Bravo and order delivery?" I ask as my eyes grow heavy, but a grin sweeps my face. Katie nods with excitement as a drunken smile falls on her lips. I wrap my arm around her neck as she does the same to me, and into the complex we go, straight up to my apartment.

"Shit." I giggle as I slam the foyer wall with the side of my body. "Steady...steady..."

"Oh...Hi Rhett." Katie says sharply, almost like when you mimic someone out of spite.

I find it hard to control my laughter. After we had the second bucket filled with liquor is when Katie dived into a ***Go Fuck Yourself, Rhett*** campaign and told me I deserved the absolute best and nothing less — I happily hopped on board.

Right now, she's not too fond of him, so I've got to usher her into my room quickly.

"Should we get chicken fingers?" I ask, still giggling as I push her towards my bedroom door.

"Fuck yes, but I'm gonna go to the bathroom first and send Ford a picture. He's been asking for —" She replies, still slurring every word before I cut her off.

I do not need an explanation of what he wants to see from her after drinks. I laugh and motion for her to go into my room herself before I turn around and stumble to get myself a glass of water.

"You look like you guys had fun today," Rhett says with a sly smile.

"Yup," I say very briefly with my back turned to him. A hiccup escapes my mouth immediately after. I fill up my cup with water from the refrigerator as I lean on it for balance.

"Ford said he wanted me to stay here until they get back tonight, so it looks like I'm sleeping over!" Katie yells excitedly as she exits my bedroom and meets me in the kitchen.

I smile at her and crinkle my nose before raising my hands and dancing to an imaginary beat in my head.

"Maybe Jacob will want to come over and keep me company when you leave my bed." I giggle as I raise my eyebrows up and down. I don't mean it, but I wanted to say it loud enough in front of Rhett — hoping he feels a little jealous somewhere inside of him.

"Yes!" She squeals.

"Have fun tonight." I say sarcastically to Rhett over my shoulder as Katie and I walk into my bedroom.

As we sit on my bed, I grab my remote to flip through to Bravo while Katie looks at her phone.

"I really like your brother." She says with a soft smile as she leans her head on my shoulder.

"I think he really likes you too, Katie." I say quietly as I lean my head on top of hers.

"I'm starving." She says, then laughs.

"Me too." I match her tone as I lift my head and grab my phone to order us dinner. "Chicken fingers, pizza, or caviar?" I laugh.

"What?" She giggles and snorts.

I don't know why we're laughing, nor do I care — this is the most fun I've had in a really long time, and she's doing the absolute best to keep my mind off of everything horrible in my life.

"All of them?" She suggests.

"Deal." I say with a nod as my eyes pool with water. I've been laughing so hard that my reflex tears kick in and stream down my cheeks. I wipe my face with the sleeves of my hoodie and order a pepperoni pizza, chicken fingers with homemade potato chips, and Siberian Sturgeon Caviar.

As soon as our order is placed, a soft knock comes from the door before it opens slightly.

"Katie?" Ford asks gently.

"Ah!" Katie giddily yells as she throws a pillow off of her lap and jumps out of my bed.

She meets Ford at my door, and they kiss...multiple times. It only takes the second peck on the lips before I fall on my side and bury my face in a pillow and groan. I'm happy for them, but Jesus Christ, I don't want to see this. I can't imagine how Ford feels — his brain is probably permanently scarred with seeing Rhett *literally inside of me*.

"Do you girls want to come out with us?" Ford asks, somewhat reluctantly.

"I think we've had enough drinks for today." Katie whispers.

I raise my hand with my face still buried in a pillow, only to acknowledge that I wholeheartedly agree with her. The only thing I'm looking forward to is eating, watching trash tv, and going to sleep before they get back, so I don't have to know if Rhett does bring anyone home.

Once Katie is done loving up on Ford, she resumes her position on my bed after I lift myself up. It's only another thirty minutes before all of our food arrives, and I couldn't be happier.

"You have to fucking try this." I say with wide eyes as I spoon caviar on a potato chip. "I swear to God, Katie. Look me in my eyes. I swear to God, this is the best thing I've ever tasted." I hold up the chip to her lips as she opens her mouth, and I place it on her tongue.

"Holy fuck." She says with a mouth full as her hand scoops under her mouth to not make a mess.

"Right?"

"Make me another," she demands, "And try it with this." She says as she holds a slice of pizza up.

I scoop the caviar again with a plastic spoon and slide it on a chip before I feed it to her and take the pizza out of her hands. I scoop another large spoonful and put it on the end of the pizza before I take a bite.

"Christ." I say as I chew. "This is it." I nod.

As Below Deck plays on my TV, we divulge in one hundred and fifty dollars worth of caviar, putting it on everything we have. Somewhere between the last slice of pizza and the last bit of chips, we fall asleep sitting up and leaning on each other.

I only know because my eyes slowly open when Katie's phone starts buzzing. I assume it's Ford and shut my eyes again as she quietly slips out of my room and shuts the door. I try to fall back asleep, but the light from my TV shining is too bright. I pat my hands blindly around my bed to feel for the remote, only trying for ten seconds before I get agitated and sit up fully. I lean over, grab the control from my nightstand, and power off the TV before I flip the covers of my bedspread over me. With my room silent now, I can hear voices in the living area, a woman's voice and a man's voice. My eyes flutter shut again before I hear a knocking noise — it's not a knocking at my door. It's more like someone knocking on wood or a wall.

I groan as I push my head further into my pillow to muffle out the noise, only to have my eyes spring open once I hear moaning. There's no way Katie and Ford would be screwing in the living room instead of his own bedroom, which can only mean one thing.

I sit up instantly and quietly drift my legs to the side of the bed before I tip-toe on the hardwood to press my ear on my bedroom door. I hear it again, a woman moaning quietly. I carefully twist open my doorknob without making a single sound or creak, then proceed to tip-toe around a slight corner that blocks off my view of the living room — and that's when I see it.

My heart falls, finding rock bottom in the pit of my belly, leaving only a space where it used to be while a sharp breath escapes my lungs.

I feel sick to my fucking stomach.

Like everything in my body is about to expel right here, right now, and I have no way of keeping it down. There is no way I can stop the small gasp that comes from my throat.

Rhett's eyes move away from the blonde riding him on the couch and lock with me.

"Fuck." He says as he pushes the blonde off of him and stands up. "Emilia." He says in a desperate tone as he covers himself with his hand, not quickly enough for me to notice he is actually wearing a condom with this one.

For a moment, I can't breathe. I look at the blonde before my eyes fixate back on his. I can't stop the tears from welling up and immediately turn around to my bedroom and slam the door shut before I lock it behind me.

"Emilia." Rhett says from the other side of my door while he pounds on it.

I hear the woman's voice again, this time more clear, and it's hard not to notice the anger in her tone.

I walk to my bed and fall face-first onto it as I cry into my pillow. I don't know why I'm surprised. It's Rhett. Why did I think I would be any different to him than some slut he met at a club? Why did I think that the look in his eyes when he was fucking me looked a hell of a lot like love? Why did I think for one second this man could possibly have feelings for me when he doesn't have any feelings *at all*?

I hear the front door slam shut, and not long after, a soft knock comes from my door. The tears keep falling from my cheeks as I ignore the sound. He only knocks one more time before the entire apartment falls silent. Maybe an hour or two passes before I eventually tire myself out from crying and drift back to sleep.

I wish I could go back.

Back to the days when I didn't see Rhett Adler the way I see him now. To the days he tormented, bullied, and teased me — *not* in a good way.

It was like, one day — a flip switched, and I saw him in a different light.

The problem is, *I can't go back.*

I can't see him any differently.

Clearly, he doesn't want me, and I have to live with that. So — I'll be stuck here, in love with him silently, until my mind can erase every trace of him.

Chapter 20

Emilia

I've been sitting in my bed this morning for thirty minutes in the same position. My legs are to my chest as my arms bear hug around them, and I squeeze tight while my head rests on my knees.

When I was thirteen, my mother paid for acting classes for me. I think she thought I wanted to be some star because of how obsessed I was with Disney Channel. If anything — it shows how little she knew about me. I didn't want to be an actress but learned some useful things that year. I feel I can act like nothing is wrong while being completely distressed inside. Sure, it's not a way to live, but until I find someone who makes me feel every bit of alive as he does...I'll be stuck in this tortured purgatory.

I throw on black sweatpants and a matching sports bra before I toss my hair up in a messy ponytail and walk to the kitchen to put my minimal acting skills to the test. Katie and Ford stand in the kitchen, and out of the corner of my eye, I see Rhett's figure sitting on the couch.

"Good morning." I say cheerfully to Katie and Ford.

The hardest part is faking a smile, but from recent events at work, I think I've nailed it down now.

"Good morning." They say back.

"Do you want some coffee?" Ford asks with his back turned to me.

"Please," I say as I walk closer to Katie. "Can I talk to you for a moment?" I smile at Katie while I reach to grab her arm.

"Yeah, of cour—"

"Great!" I say as I yank her arm to follow me towards my bedroom.

Once we are inside, I shut the door softly before I turn to look at her. At that moment, the smile slips from my face.

"What's wrong?" She asks.

"Rhett was fucking someone else last night. I walked out into the living room and saw it." I say after I take a deep breath to prepare myself from reliving it.

"I'm sorry…" She trails off. "What did he do when he saw you?" She asks.

"He threw her off of him."

"He threw her?"

"Yeah — he literally tossed her to the side and stood up immediately."

"How were they fucking?"

"She was riding him."

"Riding him?"

"Yes. Katie. She was on top of him, bouncing up and down like a fucking rag doll and moaning like an amateur porn star." I spit out.

Katie grimaces as her jaw clenches, just thinking about the site of it all. "What did his face look like?"

"His what?"

"His face…did he look like he was enjoying it? Did you see his face?" She asks.

"His face…yeah, I mean, I saw him…" I say, trying to remember. "He looked — bored." I say flatly at the realization.

"Is that how he normally looks…with you?" She asks gently.

"No." I softly say.

"What did he do after he threw her off of him?"

"Well...I ran to my room because I started crying like a fucking idiot. He just kept calling my name, like he wanted to talk, but it was hardly the time. I just ignored him, and that was it." I explain.

Katie nods slowly as her bottom lip pulls into her mouth, staying secure from her teeth biting down. She looks as if she's assessing or just processing the information.

"What are you going to do now?" She asks with a gentle expression.

"I'm gonna...try to move on." I sigh. "Hopefully, he can find a place soon, then, he will be out of here, and I won't have to see him every day."

"What if he doesn't find a place soon?" She asks.

"I am just going to...act like everything is okay."

"Even though it's not?"

"That's life, Katie." I say as my eyes become glossy.

She grins sympathetically as she pulls me in for a hug. She wraps me in her arms, and I take a deep breath, only allowing one singular tear to fall before I exhale again and break away from her grasp. I wipe the tear off my cheek with the palm of my hand and flash her a smile.

"I need coffee," I say before we both leave my bedroom and walk back to the kitchen.

Ford and Rhett are now sitting on the stools by the island while they eat their breakfast. I grab the coffee Ford made for me and take a sip.

"Emilia, can you make something good for dinner tonight?" Ford asks as I have my back turned to him. I spin around and grin slightly at both of them.

"What do you guys want?" I ask as sweetly as I can.

Rhett looks at me with a heavyhearted expression.

"Tacos?" Ford asks as he turns to Rhett.

"That sounds good," Rhett says in a deep tone after he clears his throat.

"Katie...do you want to stay for dinner?" Ford asks her. I turn to her and nod my head yes.

"Yeah, that sounds great, but Emilia and I were going to go out afterward."

"We were?" I ask quietly before she cuts me off.

"But I can come back and stay the night with you again if you want." She says as she links her arm with Ford's and kisses him on the cheek.

He grins cheekily with his eyes closed before he agrees to her. I'm unaware of our plans to go out, but I'm assuming she has some idea to help me get out of this apartment. I quickly glance at Rhett before I take another sip of my coffee. His eyes seem destructive, mixed with emotions but still as blue as the middle of an ocean. I don't know what he's thinking or feeling, but I have to stop caring.

I need to.

For my own sanity.

A backless mini-dress is the sluttiest thing I could find in my closet. Since the entire day, including dinner, went smoothly with me slapping a happy attitude on, I feel even more confident that I can successfully move on from whatever the fuck this was between Rhett and me.

"You almost ready?" Katie asks as she peeks her head through my bedroom door.

"Done." I say as I finish clasping my strappy black heels on and stand up straight. "Ah, shit, hold on." I say as I dig through the top drawer of my dresser and pull out small gold earrings. I shove them in and grab a mini clutch next to my tv before I nod my head at her.

"Let's go." She smiles as we walk into the kitchen. Both boys are in the living room watching football as Katie says goodbye. I stay silent as we continue to walk out.

"Maybe you should see if Jacob wants to come out tonight." She says as we almost enter the foyer. I grin while my chin is still tilted downwards. *I* know what she's doing

— *she* knows what she's doing — and I'm thankful... *for her.*

"I have the perfect bar I want to take you to. Craft cocktails, good music, you're going to love it." Katie says excitedly as we climb into our Uber.

"I'm so ready. I need all of the drinks." I laugh.

Our ride is short, but walking is an absolute no for Katie when she's wearing heels. She wants to move as minimally as possible. She hates heels, she hates anything that isn't flats, and I'm absolutely fine with that.

Our driver pulls to the side of the road, and as I look out the window, I can't tell where in the world this place is. It's small and short compared to the skyscrapers on either side. No extra signage or flashy lights. We both climb out on my side, and I follow her through the doors of the gray brick building. The lighting inside is dark, while the entire place feels more like it came from the Prohibition Era. Secluded, cozy, and full of deep red tones. The bartender greets Katie and me as we take a seat and he grabs us two cocktail menus for us to look at — it only takes my eyes a moment to adjust before I can see the page clearly. Katie and I glance for a moment and discuss what sounds good.

"I'll take a Pisco Sour, please." I say with a grin.

"And a Clover Club for me, please." Katie says right after me.

"Coming right up." The bartender says with an open-mouthed smile.

"Cute, right?" Katie asks.

"Him?" I say as I point my thumb in the bartender's direction.

"No," she laughs. "This place."

"Oh...yes. Very cute." I giggle.

It's only a moment before our drinks are set in front of us. Katie's is pretty and pink with raspberries on top pierced with a skewer. Mine is of a yellow tone with some kind of foam on top.

"Cheers." I smile as I raise my glass to Katie.

"Cheers babes." She says as she clinks my glass.

The tartness and sweetness mixed in my drink make my lips pucker, but after my second sip, I'm used to it — and after the second glass, it goes down a lot quicker.

"Ford texted me." Katie says as she pulls her phone out of her purse. I take another sip and set my glass down as I look at her. "He said he and Rhett are going out too." She says gently. My stomach knots at the thought of another last night, but I can't care anymore.

I just can't let myself.

"You should see if Jacob wants to come here." Katie suggests.

I'm sure my expression has shifted, and that's what gave her the idea. I let the proposition simmer momentarily before pulling out my phone.

ASSHOLE RHETT ADLER: Em, can we talk later?

and

JACOB DE LUCA: Got any plans tonight?

My heart races seeing Rhett's name, but I quickly swipe it away and message Jacob instead.

EMILIA: I'm at The Library in West Loop with Katie. Want to come?

JACOB DE LUCA: I'll be there in fifteen.

"Well...he'll be here soon." I say to Katie as I put my phone back into my clutch.

"Good!" She says excitedly to me as she shakes my arm back and forth. "Can we have another round?" She asks the bartender as he passes by us.

We sip our drinks and talk about anything but the work coming for us this week. We both have multiple deadlines to get through, so we decide that if we act like they're nonexistent, we can at least save some sanity until then.

The door opens to The Library, and I turn my head to see Jacob walking in. His stature is tall, and the baseball cap on his head matches the hoodie underneath his jacket. I smile and turn my body to quickly hop off the barstool and wrap my arms around his neck as he hugs me around my waist.

"Jacob — Katie, Katie — Jacob." I say as I formally introduce them to one another.

"Nice to meet you...again." He says as he shakes her hand.

I position myself back on my seat as Jacob takes the one next to me.

"What are you ladies drinking?" He asks.

I hand him a menu and tell him what we got, I opt for him to choose another one so I can try it. He quickly agrees and smiles wide. I know he's been wanting to get back into my pants as soon as he could, sharing drinks at least gets his lips on the same rim as mine.

"Jesus, I forgot how hot he was." Katie whispers in my ear as I lean closer to her.

I chuckle once as my lips curl up in a smile. He definitely is very nice to look at, I agree.

"So, Jacob, what do you do for a living?" Katie asks.

"I help my dad run his restaurant." He says so matter-of-factly.

"Cool!" She says, trying to sound excited. "Is that what you've always wanted to do?"

"No." He laughs. "If I had the choice, I would just not work. I'd rather travel the world and not be tied down to one spot." He says with a grin.

Oh boy.

"Hm...interesting," Katie says, sounding anything but interested.

Hopefully, now she sees why I never thought this would be a good fit.

"Do you want kids someday?" Katie blurts out.

"Jesus, Katie," I mumble, choking back a laugh.

"Someday. Maybe. I'm not sure. I guess it just depends. I want to do and see a lot of things before that time comes." Jacob laughs. "Maybe, like, when I'm forty or something."

"Yeah, I get it," I say, even though I totally don't. I'd be married with five kids right now if it were up to me.

"Penicillin, sir." The bartender says as he sets Jacob's drink in front of him.

"It's so pretty!" I say, excited I get to try blended scotch.

"You want the first sip?" Jacob asks as he holds his drink to me with a smirk.

I slowly lift my eyes to him as a sly grin forms on my face. I grab the drink and take a small sip. The smoky flavor hits me immediately, as does the scotch floater on top. I cough as my nose wrinkles and hand him back his drink.

"I think I drank all the scotch on top." I laugh, as does he and Katie.

He takes a sip and doesn't flinch.

"It's actually really good." He says.

As the night continues, Jacob keeps Katie and me engaged in conversation, something he's very good at. He's extroverted, doesn't seem shy whatsoever, easy to chat with, that's for sure. After a couple of hours of drinking, we have pretty strong buzzes, and I decide that now is a great time to go home…and he's coming with me.

He's not my *Mr. Right* by any means, but he makes a pretty good *Mr. Right Now*.

Chapter 21
Emilia

"Good night." I say to Katie as Jacob and I hold hands and walk into my bedroom. The boys aren't home yet, so if Rhett brings anyone back, I won't have to see it. Hopefully, I'll be too preoccupied inside my own room.

"I'm glad you came out tonight." I say to Jacob as he sits on the edge of my bed.

"Thanks for inviting me." He says as he stretches his arms out for me to fit inside of them.

I lean in and hug him as he nestles his head between my shoulder and jaw.

"You smell so good." He says as he buries his face in my hair and gently kisses my neck.

I sigh at the feeling and tilt my head a little further. His fingers lightly trace down my spine, and his touch feels almost like ice across my bare skin.

"This dress looks really good on you too." He says softly as he kisses my neck again.

I whimper slightly and run my fingers through the hair on the back of his head. He lays his tongue flat against my skin and lightly nibbles at my neck as he gently pushes my dress straps off my shoulders.

I roll my eyes as my head falls back, now wearing nothing but a grin as my dress falls to the floor. He sighs as his hands come to my breasts, squeezing and lightly massaging them with his gentle touch. He dips his head down and sweeps my nipple into his warm mouth. The heat from his breath bounces off of my skin as his tongue flicks back and forth. I moan quietly as my head falls back again, and the waves in his hair intertwine with my fingers. I hear the front door shut but don't pay any mind to it. I want to feel him more.

I push his head into me as he sucks and flicks my nipple before his mouth comes to mine. He gently kisses me as his hand holds the side of my face.

"Lay down." He says softly.

I do as I'm told and step out of my dress before laying on my bed beside him. He stands up and positions himself between my legs while he grabs my hips and pulls me to make my waist even with the edge of the bed. He kneels down and gently kisses my inner thigh a couple of times before placing his mouth fully on my pussy. A moan escapes from my lips as his tongue works on me, and just as he glides his tongue along my slit, a soft knock sounds on my door.

"Emilia?" Rhett's voice whispers through.

Both of our heads shoot to the door, and my breathing becomes rapid and heavy like a thirty-pound weight is sitting on my chest.

"Keep going." I whisper to Jacob as I look back at him.

His mouth resides back on me as his tongue glides up my slit gently. He lightly flicks his tongue on my clit before I push his head into me further and grind my hips.

Another knock sounds from my door.

"Emilia?" Rhett says again, this time a little louder.

"Not a good time." I say loud enough for him to hear on the other side, my voice slightly strained from the groan that wants to push through.

I buck my hips into Jacob to apply more pressure on his tongue. He's too gentle, too soft...if I have any shot of coming tonight, he'll have to work a little harder.

"Put your fingers in." I demand quietly.

"What?" Jacob says as he lifts up from me slightly.

"Put your fingers inside of me." I say as I grab his hand from my leg and push it between my thighs.

His mouth falls back on my clit as two of his fingers slide gently inside of me. A moan I was trying to hold back breaks through my lips, and not a second longer goes by before a loud pounding erupts on my door.

"Emilia, open your door." Rhett demands.

"Keep going." I whisper to Jacob as his fingers thrust inside of me.

Another moan escapes me, this one louder than the rest, and without hesitation, my door breaks open. The trim nearly breaks free with it as Rhett stands in the doorway. An enraged expression is cast upon his face as Jacob's head darts up from in between my thighs.

"Get the fuck up." Rhett demands to Jacob as he storms into my room.

"Rhett!" I yell as I prop myself up.

"What the hell?" Jacob shouts.

"I said get the fuck up!" Rhett screams as he grabs Jacob by the sweatshirt and stands him up.

"Rhett, stop!" I shout at him.

"What the hell is going on?" Ford says as he rushes to my room. "Jesus Christ!" He yells as he sees me, yet again, naked inside *my own* bedroom. Katie runs behind him, but by the time she sees, I already have my throw blanket draped over me.

"Rhett, knock it off!" I yell.

"Get the hell out of here." Rhett says as he yanks Jacob's sweatshirt towards the door.

Jacob pushes him in the chest with both hands — the force alone makes Rhett stumble backward and unleash his grasp on him. Rhett's eyes fill with fury as his lips press together and his jaw clenches. Rhett shoves Jacob in the chest twice as hard, and in an instant, both men are throwing fists at each other.

"Stop!" Ford yells as he tries to get in between both of them.

I stand up and scream at them both, hoping my efforts will help as well. Fists are flying while Ford tries to dodge them. Jacob lands a punch on Rhett's face, but no more than a second passes before Rhett's fist makes contact with Jacob's eye.

Grunts, screams, and curse words fill the apartment, and I'm sure the entire building can hear what is happening inside this room. Ford wedges enough space between both of them before he guides Jacob outside of my door, and I look at Katie with nothing less than terror written on my face. She grabs a hold of Jacob and walks him out of sight and out of the apartment.

"What in the fuck is going on?" Ford shouts to Rhett and me, as I stand in nothing but a cream herringbone blanket around my bare naked body.

Rhett blows out a loud breath as his hands rub back and forth on his head.

"I — I couldn't let that happen." Rhett stammers with a fire still in his eyes.

"Why the fuck not?" Ford yells in his face.

"Because... I fucking love her, Ford!" Rhett screams back at him.

"What?" Ford shouts.

"I love her! I've... *been* in love with her."

"Since when?"

"I don't know — since, since Miami."

"Miami? She was fucking sixteen, Rhett. You were almost twenty!" Ford shouts.

I stay completely still and in shock, with only my jaw slightly agape — dumbfounded at what I'm hearing. The only thing that has changed is the rapid pace of my heartbeat and the disbelief that runs through my veins.

"I know." Rhett says calmly. "I know!" He says louder. "We...didn't do anything, not until I came here." He explains.

"I don't — I don't want to hear this." Ford cuts him off.

Silence falls between the thick air, and I quickly steal Katie's glance now that she's back. The horror on her face matches mine equally.

"Well then, what in the fuck happened in Miami, and why have you never told me?" Ford asks.

It's as if these two have forgotten there is anyone else in the room.

"I don't know. I can't explain it. Can I — can I just clean myself up?" Rhett says as he brings his fingers to his top lip, only touching lightly before the blood transfers to the tips of them.

"You need to leave." Ford demands quietly.

Silence falls between them, and neither move an inch.

"How about we sleep at my place tonight?" Katie suggests softly as she tugs on Ford's arm.

Ford looks at me, appalled and with a stiffened jaw, before he looks at Rhett the same way. It only takes a moment, and an exaggerated breath from Ford before he and Katie walk out into the living room, with only another minute before the front door slams shut behind them. Rhett's body twitches at the sound.

Rhett finally turns his head to me, and in the same moment, I see the blood drip down his chin.

"Go sit in there," I say gently, pointing to my bathroom.

He moves slowly, and I drop the blanket around me before I pick up an old T-shirt and boy shorts from my floor. I walk into the bathroom to see Rhett sitting on my toilet. His back is leaned against the tank, and his arms rest between his legs. The bloodstream on his face flows from his top lip to the bottom of his chin, dripping on his white t-shirt. I look at him for a moment, completely benumb before grabbing a washcloth from the cabinet and running it under cool water. I walk over to Rhett and slowly kneel between his legs. He sits up straight, and I dab the washcloth gently on his cut — a loud exhale pushes through his nose, and I move it away from his upper lip so I can clean the rest of the blood off his face.

"What in the hell just happened..." I whisper as my eyes remain focused on cleaning him up.

"I don't know," he replies. "I'm — I'm really sorry."

"You broke my door," I say as I wipe the last of the blood away, only dabbing lightly at the cut now.

"I only broke your door because I knew I could fix it." He says as his lips curl upwards slightly in a grin.

A small smile eases my face but only for a moment until I realize.

"Was all of that true — what you said?" I say softly.

"Yeah." He breathes. His tone is more gruff than normal. His gaze still locks with mine and I swallow the lump that was lodged in my throat.

"I'm... in love with you, Emilia. I have been for a really long time." His voice remains low and soft.

I let his words fill my body and swarm in the lower cavity of my stomach. All of his actions, everything he has said to me during all of these years, flood through my brain only to try to make sense of it all. I can see — the way he always made it a purpose to do something special for my birthday. — the way he knows my favorite foods, down to what I order. All of these pieces fit together like some fucked up puzzle.

"What happened in Miami?" I ask.

"It was when you were dating that douchebag I told you was a drug dealer. He left you at some restaurant on Fort Lauderdale beach. You didn't want to call your brother, so you called me to come to pick you up. Before we went home, you wanted to walk across the street to see how warm the ocean felt at night, so I followed you. We stayed on the beach that night for over two hours, and... I'll never forget it. I think the specific moment was when you were dancing on the shoreline, the water was splashing up from your feet, and you were wearing that bright pink bikini and my white button down shirt I gave you to cover up with. You also wore that shark tooth necklace you *had to have*—"

"It was Florida...I thought it was only customary." I interject quietly.

"Well...that was it. That was when I first fell in love with you." He says.

My breaths become short as I try to relax my pulse. I remember the night perfectly, and I took his attitude for being a prude and boring. He was sitting in the sand, with his arms behind him for support just staring at me. I wanted him to get in and feel the water, but he refused. I shrugged him off, not even giving it a second thought.

My eyelids flutter, and I lean up further to reach his face. With my hands on his knees, I lightly kiss his lips, only to try not to hurt his wound. He breathes into me and kisses me back. I kiss him once more, only a gentle peck, as his lips part slightly for me, and his hand cups my face. His tongue gently grazes my top lip, and I pull away.

"Why haven't you said anything? All these years...why haven't you told me?" I ask as the thought hits me.

"Ford is my best friend. I didn't want him to hate me. You weren't even eighteen yet, Emilia. I was almost twenty. That's insane." He explains.

"Well...what about when I was eighteen?" I ask.

"Emilia...I have — I have to tell you something." He says as his eyebrows burrow and the corners of his mouth drop. It's almost like the color of his complexion drains from his cheeks at whatever it is he needs to say.

"Having kids is really important to you. I've known this about you for a really long time. I am so in love with you that I knew if I said anything or did anything with you — I would never want to let you go. Emilia... I can't have kids...I can't...reproduce. I will never be able to give you the one thing you truly desire. There is no way I could ever make you fully happy." He says.

I sit on my heels as my eyes become pools of water. I don't know what I expected to hear...but this was not it.

I don't know how to process this.

I don't know what to think.

I remain still, only blinking once, which forces a tear to escape.

"I don't...date other women. I don't bother having feelings for anyone else, not yet, at least. I knew eventually I had to say something to you. I couldn't keep it bottled up, and that night, that I watched you...and that fucking loser, I, I couldn't stop. I couldn't look away. I wished that could be me. Emilia, I knew once I fucked you, I wouldn't be able to stop. It's so easy with everyone else. To not get involved, to just fuck. I needed you to move on from me. I kept it going because I couldn't stop, and when Ford finally caught us, I knew it really had to be the end. I tried to get you to move on, I only brought that girl back to make Ford happy, and I thought, maybe if he had told you the next day — it would be easier for you to be with someone else too. I couldn't be cold to you, Emilia, I couldn't even pretend to hate you if I tried. But once you moved on tonight...I couldn't handle it. It's not fair to you. I will be out of here by tomorrow. I know I'm just making you even more confused and I'm so sorry, Emilia."

My chin quivers, and the tears from my eyes roll down my face as I wipe them away with my fingertips. My breath trembles just like the beating in my chest.

"Will you sleep with me tonight?" Is all I manage to choke out.

He stands up slowly with me and we walk to my bed. The door to my bedroom is nearly hanging on by two screws while the trim remains popped off. Rhett climbs under the covers, and I scoot my body closer to his he wraps his arm around me and pulls me in tighter, so our noses are almost touching.

"I will always love you, Emilia." He whispers as he kisses the tip of my nose.

I run my fingers over his short hair and grab his neck as I gently push my lips on his. He kisses me back, and our lips press together harder. The next kiss I give him, my tongue follows and sweeps inside his parted lips. His grip squeezes around me as his tongue dives inside my mouth this time, and we continue back and forth, taking turns on whose tongue fights to get in. He presses his body against mine, and I can feel him, solid, hard, beneath his sweatpants. I wrap my leg around him and bring him closer to me to feel him between my thighs. As I kiss him, I roll my hips to glide up and down his length. Between the tears from my cheeks and the blood from his lip, my mouth tastes like a salty penny, and I feel like I'm drunk and high at the same time.

I slow down our kisses and stop grinding my hips as I pull away slightly, only to look him in the eyes.

"I love you too, Rhett..." I whisper as my hot breath mixes with his. "But I don't know if we can keep doing this." I say as the tears well again in my eyes.

As much as I want him and need him, I don't know how we can move forward. I have to decide between everything I'd ever hoped for in life — or him, and I can't make that choice tonight.

He presses his lips together as he swallows slowly, only letting out a small sigh from his nose as he nuzzles me into his chest and holds me... secure and warm, all wrapped up in him until I fall asleep.

Chapter 22

Rhett

I lean on the back wall of the elevator. My arms crossed while I lock my jaw tight.

I left before she woke up. I don't think Ford and I could have repaired anything between us if he had come home and saw me sleeping next to her this morning. We would have fought, *fist-fought*, I just know it. I know him, and the best thing I can do right now is give him space.

I love Emilia — with every fiber of my being. I'm happiest when she's around. Truthfully, life is shitty without her. I've held back for so long. It was easy at first to block it out, block *her* out. But every time we would part ways, even for a short while...I realized how bleak, how bland, and how fucking miserable my life is without her.

I can't possibly ever make her fully happy. I thought I was being helpful by not getting involved with her for her sake. She's been drunk, before she turned twenty-one, and whether she realizes it or not — she's told me how she's felt about me, *really*, felt about me.

When she was nineteen — we all went to a house party. Later in the night, Ford went off in a bedroom with one of the girls that lived there, and Emilia and I kept drinking. After some time and a few rounds of beer pong, Emilia asked me to help her find the bathroom. We went upstairs to look when she noticed a higher loft; naturally, she wanted to explore and walked up, only to find a window with access to the roof. She called me up, and before I knew it, we were climbing out of the window with our drinks to sit and look at the stars. Eventually, we both laid down because finding the Big Dipper with our necks kinked like that was less than comfortable. We laughed and talked, and she told me she had dreams about fucking me. I played it off — like that was gross, and she turned over to face me, leaning up on her elbow while her eyes pierced through mine, letting every strand of her salty beach waved hair flow with the breeze. She told me she could see us getting married, starting a family, living happily ever after in some white picket fence dream. She said she wanted to wake up with me every day, sit at our dining table, and have our morning cup of coffee, *together*. She wanted to sit across that same table, figuring out how to do our taxes, *together*. She said she wanted to fold our laundry, take our dogs on walks, our kids to the park...together.

All of it.

She wanted to do all of these mundane things... *with me*.

I couldn't help but laugh when my heart was pounding through my chest. Of course, this was all great to hear, but how could I tell Emilia...the woman born to be a mother, that I loved her but couldn't give her children.

I understand science, we could go through numerous treatments and possibly be successful, but that is not something I want her to go through. Between the side effects and the possible emotional trauma, that's the last thing I would ever want her to experience *because of me*.

She didn't remember a drop from the roof conversation the next day, and I never brought it up. That's when I decided that I wouldn't tell her my feelings, and I left it alone.

"I'll take a *Caffe Americano* please," I say to the barista at a coffee shop down the block.

I figured I'd wait the morning out then try to call Ford and talk, but I'm getting more impatient by the second that passes. As soon as the barista hands me my coffee, I sit at a small table by the front window.

I know I need to talk to Emilia too. I can't imagine that any of this is easy for her.

I just — I just need one last night with her.

If this is it...I need to feel her one more time.

Smell her one more time.

Taste her one more time.

Chapter 23

Emilia

The front door shutting wakes me up. Ford's groan comes next. I shoot up in bed and notice Rhett is missing. Ford stares at me through my open door only for a moment before he walks to his room. I scramble out of bed and grab a pair of jeans from my dresser drawer and follow him. I knock softly on the door and can only hope he's had enough sleep and coffee for the conversation I'm about to have with him.

"What do you want?" He says in a rough tone.

"Can we... get some breakfast? Please?" I plead softly. "Just us."

His eyes drop to his feet before he looks back at me and walks out of his bedroom. I follow him as he grabs the apartment keys, and the entire walk down to the lobby and out the door to the nearest restaurant is the most silent we have ever been with each other. The *second* most silent we have ever been with each other is when I accidentally killed his hamster, *allegedly*.

But this is apparently worse for him.

We round the corner and stop at *Lola's*. We stand in line, slowly making our way inside the doors as each party before us is seated.

Still, without saying a word.

"How many?" The hostess asks us. I wait for Ford to speak, but he doesn't.

"Two, please." I say after an awkward pause.

"Right this way." She smiles as she walks us to a corner table. "Your server will be right with you." She says as she places our menus down.

We sit, and immediately he picks up his menu without so much of a glance toward me.

"Ford."

"What." He snaps as his eyes pierce mine.

"Are you seriously going to be mad at me right now?" I snarl.

"You guys fucked more than once and lied about it, Emilia. I'm not too fucking happy right now."

"You know, Ford, just because William was never a father doesn't mean you have to be mine. And who fucking cares? I'm an adult. I can sleep with whoever I want!" I snap, getting the attention of the table over.

I glance quickly at them and grimace.

"Good morning, you two, my names Laura, and I'll be your server today. Can I get you started on something to drink?" Our waitress says right when she approaches our table.

"Hi." I grin. "Can I get a vanilla latte?"

"I'll just take a regular coffee, black, please." Ford says with pressed lips and a pissed-off expression.

Our waitress nods and leaves, and my eyes fixate back on his.

"So what if I had sex with him a hundred times, Ford?"

"So what? He's my best fucking friend, Emilia, you know how he is, and he doesn't want the same things as you."

"And what do I want, huh?" I demand.

"You want a husband, Emilia. You want a family. Neither of those things Rhett will give you."

"Why do you think he's incapable of giving me those things?"

"Have you met the fucking man?" He scowls.

"Are we ready to order?" Our waitress returns with our coffees.

"Sorry," I say as I frantically open the menu. "Can I just have French toast please." I say quickly.

"I'll take the same." Ford says.

We hand our menus to her and wait until she's gone before we resume where we left off.

"And what the hell happened in Miami between you two?" He asks once the coast is clear.

"You remember that guy, Dante, I was dating?"

"The drug dealer?"

"He wasn't a — regardless, he left me at that hookah lounge restaurant we would go to,"

"That fucking prick..." Ford interjects.

"Anyways." I demand with wide eyes as I cut him off. "He left me there, and I obviously couldn't get back home because I didn't have a car,"

"Well, you never bothered to get your license..."

"Ford, please!" I beg. "Let me finish." I pause and wait for any other comments that may want to escape from him before continuing. "I called Rhett because I knew if I called you, you would beat the shit out of him before you beat the shit out of me. Rhett came to get me, and I begged him to let me feel the ocean before we went home. He said that was the night it happened. He was sitting in the sand, watching me dance and spin in the ocean, and he said…he fell in love with me right then and there." My tone becomes softer as I finish.

Ford clears his throat before he takes a sip of coffee, and his phone buzzes on the table near his hand.

"It's Rhett." He states.

I stare at him as he examines his phone and try to get any indication of what it says by the reflection in his eyes. His lips press in a straight line as he types, and I can only wait. He sets the phone down and takes another sip of his coffee. My eyes become wide, and I clear my throat.

"He said he called some apartment complex and he could move in by the end of the week, but he will get a hotel until then." He says.

"No. Not yet, Ford, please. You need to talk to him." I beg.

"There's nothing to talk about right now. He came into my home, fucked my sister, assaulted a man in your room, and broke your door. I don't think I have anything nice to say to him right now."

Our waitress brings our food, but neither of us touch our plates. We sit in silence and sip our coffees like two frenemies that only meet once a month to keep up with appearances.

I can't stand this about him. He's always so tough to forgive people, forgetting that he often makes mistakes too.

"I know you care about me, and I know you care about him too. I'm just asking you to talk with him...that's all. I'm really sorry for putting a wedge between you two. It was not intentional." I say gently.

Ford's eyes drop to his hands that are folded in front of him. His lips still press together with force, like he's biting his tongue from lashing out.

We sit in silence, with nothing else to discuss. He won't change his mind, and I can't make him. Neither of us touched our food so we get to-go boxes, knowing damn well neither of us like leftovers and these will sit in our refrigerator for a week.

"I'm not going back yet. I'll see you later." Ford mumbles as we walk out of the restaurant.

I don't even bother responding before my feet are walking in the opposite direction of him. My hands freeze as I hold both boxes of food and fight off the opposing wind and bitter chill all the way back to the apartment.

As soon as I close the door and lock it behind me, I immediately can sense Rhett is gone. The apartment is quiet and the feeling of emptiness lingers in the air.

Once I get to the open space, it's confirmed. Ford's bedroom door is half opened with only a made bed in my vision, and my door is closed — but completely fixed. Left without a scratch or indication of anything that happened to it within the last twelve hours.

I hastily grab my phone without thinking and text him.

EMILIA: You didn't have to leave.

RHETT ADLER: I did.

RHETT ADLER: Before you make a decision...about us, can I please take you to dinner tonight?

RHETT ADLER: I don't know what's going to happen between Ford and me, but I never thought of the chance of losing you completely, and I'm not ready for that yet.

My heart races like it's competing for an olympic medal, and I can feel it pulsating through my skin. As his texts flood in, my eyes scan each word and every syllable.

I've already decided.

I know what's best for me and what I want. As hard as it may be, it's a choice I'm willing to make.

I simply text him ***Okay,*** because I'm not sure how else I can put into words what I'm feeling.

The front door closes, and I peer through the darkened hallway to see Ford walk in. His eyes are glued to mine, but his expression seems softer, a lot lighter than at breakfast.

"Emilia." He breathes. "I can't tell you what to do. You're a grown woman, and you can make your own choices. He is my best friend, but — I don't even want to think of this happening — if he ever hurts you, I will fucking kill him. I promise." He finally lets out.

I swallow hard. The last thing I want to do is create a barrier in their friendship, and I'm not one hundred percent confident I can predict that Rhett *won't* hurt me.

I know he's serious, and that's what scares me.

Chapter 24

Emilia

I sit on the edge of my bed like some adolescent waiting for the bus to school, constantly glancing at my phone to check the time. Rhett said he would be here at seven, and assuming it takes approximately eight minutes to get down to the lobby and out the front doors — *nine if we account for heavy traffic with the elevators* — it looks like I should be leaving right...

Now.

I sit up and grab my purse before I shut my bedroom door. Ford left to take Katie out tonight, but I am feeling a lot better about how things have left off between us.

Once I'm in the lobby, I see Rhett's figure from behind as he stands outside the front doors.

"Hey," I say softly as I approach.

His nose is a strawberry red from the cold, but he grins when he sees me — the same grin that highlights his dimples.

"You ready?" He asks as the cool air visibly escapes his mouth, and the condensation turns to fog.

I smile and nod gently as I take his arm in mine. He said the restaurant was only a block away, so I told him I could tough it out in heels. I don't know why I said that, though. I instantly regret it after I feel the cold air hit my freshly painted toenails.

The wind hits my face while we power walk, and I curl my body as close as possible to his until we arrive.

Rhett speaks with the host, and we follow her to a table positioned to the room's left. I take off my coat and drape it over the back of my chair, the hostess had asked us if we wanted to check them, but I never do — I don't trust people, and this is my favorite jacket.

"Emilia, I'm going to be honest," Rhett says as he sits down. "It's going to be really hard for me to focus on anything else other than you in that dress." His eyes darken as his hand comes up to his mouth. He brushes his bottom lip with his thumb as his elbow rests on the table.

All I can do is smile at him. The dress was intentional, and I'm glad to see it working.

"Are you hungry?" He asks as he starts to pick up the menu our waiter left.

"Starving." I grin. My eyes fill with heat as I look at him. The short sleeves on his shirt hug his biceps, and every time he wears a light color, the black in his tattoos becomes more prominent.

We order our drinks and only minutes pass before we have them.

"I have a question," I say before I take a sip of my wine.

"Yes, Emilia?"

"How come you didn't wear a condom with me, but you had one on when I saw you with that other girl?" I ask quietly as a small smirk forms at the corner of my mouth.

He clears his throat as his eyes widen. I don't think that's what he had expected to hear.

"I just...forgot."

"The real answer, please." I press.

"Can I, uh — tell you later?"

"Tell me now," I say, the small smirk still present as my posture becomes relaxed, and I bring my wine glass to my lips. I find great joy in his discomfort.

He clears his throat once more and pauses as he breathes through his nose loud enough for me to hear.

"What do you want me to say, Emilia?" He says quietly as he leans closer to me, minimizing the table space between us. "I thought about fucking you for years, masturbated about it dozens of times. I didn't want to waste a second before getting inside of you. I wanted to be as close to you as possible and feel you fully. Feel how wet you were, how tight were. I didn't pull out because you felt so fucking good. I didn't want it to end, and I wanted to watch my cum drip out of your tight little pussy." He spits out. "Is that a better answer for you?"

My thighs rage with the heat between them. Watching his lips move as he speaks about me only sends fire missiles to my stomach. The way his tongue dances in his mouth and peeks through every time he says a word with the letter *L*, only makes me want it pressed on my body that much more.

I take a sip of my wine as I part my legs slightly, only to allow myself to cool off for a moment.

"Are we ready to order?" Our waitress interrupts.

"We need another minute." I breathe, not having even bothered to look at the menu yet. "I'm going to use the restroom," I say to Rhett.

I need a moment to calm myself — there's no way I can think about eating when my body screams for him like this.

He leans back in his seat and grabs his drink while I stand up and find any signs that indicate a bathroom. As soon as I do, I walk in and immediately place my hands on the counter and turn the faucet on, only so I can run my hands under the cool water. This is the only thing I can possibly think of to make the searing temperature in my body go down. Out of the corner of my eye, I can see the bathroom door open slightly.

"Rhett?" I question as he slides into the women's restroom and leans his back on the door.

I shut the faucet off and walk up to him, ensuring each stall here is vacant on the way.

"What are you doing?" I ask as my lips curl upwards slightly.

"I'm very well aware that this may be my last night with you, and I would rather starve than not taste you one more time." He says as he steps closer to me and cups my face with his hand.

My eyes flutter shut as he slowly leans into me, and my mouth hangs agape, just waiting for him to fit his lips in with mine. He brushes against me gently, breathing into my mouth as our lips barely touch, like he's contemplating every decision he's ever made, and then his mouth swarms over mine. His tongue rolls in and sweeps inside as my hands grab his face tightly like I don't ever want to let him go. He turns me around and presses his body flush against mine until my back hits the door to keep it secure. His hands climb up my legs underneath my dress, frantic, like he can't get there fast enough. He pulls down my thong while his mouth is still moving with mine, and it only takes him a moment before he drops to his knees in front of me and lifts my leg. He bites softly at my calf as he works his way up my leg, taking little nibbles out of my skin as he applies more and more pressure. By the time he bites my inner thigh, a chill sweeps over my center that signals my clit to throb. I can already feel how wet I am by the slight dribble that runs down through the center of me to my backside.

"Jesus, Emilia." He groans as he lightly traces the tip of his finger on my slit and pulls it back to see my wetness thicker than water.

He places his hand on top of my pussy and lightly pulls it up with his thumb, exposing my clit fully to him. He looks up at me through his eyelashes as he presses his mouth on me. I see his tongue work on my slit as he nuzzles his face into my pussy, and my head falls back onto the door, my eyes rolling. I let out a quiet whimper as I drag my hand along his head, feeling the buzz of his hair and how soft it is. Between the thrill of being caught in a public restroom and how his mouth works on me, I'm not sure which will make me cum faster. He sucks and flicks at my clit so effortlessly that I have no choice but to roll my hips with pleasure. He flattens his tongue as my eyes lock back on his.

"I'm gonna cum." I whisper as I nod my head *yes*, I want him to keep going — just like that.

My hand tries to grab onto his hair but fails to catch anything between my fingers. All I can do is hold the top of his head while he works vigorously with his mouth. My body shakes, and I clench as the feeling arises. I hear him sucking as I cum, drinking all of my orgasm as it spills on his face. The convulsions fail to cease as he continues, and my core tightens like I've done a hundred crunches. He moans into my pussy until I stop shaking and set my leg firmly on the ground. My breathing doesn't slow down as I lean my entire body back on the bathroom door. He stands up and looks at me face to face. His entire mouth is wet from me. Droplets form on his cheeks, chin, and lips, and the entire lower half of his stubble is glossy. He breathes loudly as he leans into me and dips his head to kiss my lips.

"Let's go to your hotel." I breathe into him.

Chapter 25

Emilia

We both sit in the back of the Nissan our driver picked us up in as Rhett's hand drops to the inner part of my thigh, barely grazing the skin underneath my dress. A small sigh he must have heard bolts out of my mouth at the feeling of his cold touch, and his hand firmly placed on me now squeezes tightly. I remain seated forward, casually making eye contact with the driver through the rear-view mirror to avoid making him suspicious while Rhett's hand glides up even higher, disappearing under my dress. His finger traces my panty line, and I slam my legs shut, instantly trapping his hand in place. I've never gotten fingered in the back of an Uber, but I can say with most certainty it's not on my bucket list either. He laughs lightly as his head falls back on the headrest. I have no choice but to smirk when I see the dimples appearing back on his cheeks from the corner of my eye.

As soon as the car stops, Rhett and I exit as quickly as we can. I follow him through the lobby and into the elevators as he fast walks through the building, and I can't help but relish in his sense of urgency to take my clothes off. The tension between us as we wait for the elevator doors to close is thick like crystallized honey, and I swear I can feel the electricity between us as we stand almost shoulder to shoulder.

Before the elevator doors shut completely, he's already facing me with his hand on the wall behind me, pinning me there in place. He breathes into me as he grazes his lips slightly against mine, to not kiss me fully yet as he brings his other hand to my throat, only to secure me further.

"Emilia," His voice almost in a whisper as I feel the hot heat of his breath cascade on my lips.

I don't give him a second to speak anymore before my lips crash onto his. He pulls away slightly, only to lick his fingers as he stares into my soul, and drops his hand under my dress and between my thighs. All it takes is one quick motion of pushing my panties to the side before his wet fingers rub on my pussy. I moan as my mouth hangs open next to his. Both of us lean into each other as our heavy breaths mix, and my eyes start to roll back. The elevator door dings, and for the entire thirteen floors, I completely forget where we are. Rhett pulls his hand away quickly before straightening up and beside me, shoulder to shoulder again. A couple walks into the elevator as we leave, and I follow him down the hallway until we get to his door. As soon as the green light flashes, he removes the key and his hands cup my face instantly to pull me in. Our lips clash as he pushes the door open with his back. Our tongues glide against one another, and little whimpers flee from my throat as I feel his soft lips. He brings me further into the room, still with our lips glued together, and backs me into the bathroom before pulling away, only for a moment to start the bathtub.

"What are you doing?" I giggle as I watch him feel the water temperature.

The tub is large, with jets lined all along the sides, but Rhett isn't small, and his tree trunk thighs I feel will have a hard time fitting in there, especially with me in there too.

"If this is our last time fucking, Emilia...I want to make it special." He says as he stands up straight and lifts his shirt over his head.

"Rhett, It's —" I try to spit out before his mouth falls back on mine, his hand reaches for my face again, and he grabs me with force while our tongues dance together.

The sound of the bathtub filling remains constant as we both try to strip each other of the clothes we're wearing, and once my dress falls to the floor, so do his pants. He breaks free and steps back to look at me... intensely, with his fingers pulling at his bottom lip as if he knows this is the last time he will see my naked body and wants to take it all in. His teeth tug at the same lip slightly as his eyes travel down the length of my body. My eyebrows pinch only lightly as a soft smile forms on my lips.

It's odd having someone admire my body like this — even with all the flaws I seem to fixate on, he makes me feel as if they don't cease to exist.

He turns around slightly to stop the water and extends his hand to me as his eyes find mine. I take my hand in his and step into the tub, one foot after the other, and he follows right behind. The initial sting of the hot water on my cold feet takes only a minute to adjust before I ease myself in and lay back as he shifts himself in between my legs. My smile doesn't fade as he grabs my foot and brings it to his lips, kissing the arch with his eyes closed. I stare, in awe of some sort, at the gentle affection as he brings my foot back down near the water and presses his thumbs in, massaging the very middle with a firm touch.

"I'm really sorry...about everything, Emilia." He says with a hushed voice. I can tell he's feeling regretful and

ALL OF IT, WITH YOU

despondent even with everything that happened and what he feels is to come.

I pull my feet towards me as I reposition myself to crawl on him, the water sloshes as I move in the tightened space and straddle him the best I can given his thighs that press against the width of the tub. I bring my hands to his face and close my eyes as I kiss him gently. His arms sweep across the small of my back, and he squeezes, not enough to hurt but enough for me to get the feeling he doesn't want to let me go, *ever*. He kisses me back, grazing his tongue against mine, and every kiss after is more prominent, more forceful. His fingernails drag along my back as his tongue glides around with mine, and I find it hard to keep my body still as my hips roll with every kiss. I whimper as he grabs the back of my neck with a firm grasp, and suddenly we're in a race to see how fast he can get inside of me. His hand falls to his cock, and I lift slightly to fit him in. The water splashes almost to my chin, and the tight area we're in doesn't make for an easy entrance. I raise just a bit more until we get it right, then ease down on him, locking my lips back with his. He bites on my bottom lip as he moves his hand to my breast, cupping it gently before brushing his thumb over my nipple. I whimper at his soft touch as I bounce lightly on him, riding him the best I can, but with the confined space and the waves of the water splashing in between us, it's proven a little too difficult.

A small giggle escapes my lips as I try to shift my leg in the awkward position, and he grins, realizing this probably wasn't the best place to try and fuck.

"Stand up." He whispers into my lips as his nose lightly grazes mine. I smile as I push myself out of the tub, carefully stepping out, so I don't slip on the white marble tile. He follows me and takes my hand as I lead us into the room. I only make it to the small couch pressed against the large windows before his arm is fully wrapped around my waist, pulling me on top of him as he sits. I laugh and squeal at the sudden jolt, and my mouth falls on his. Both of us in smiles as my hands cup his face, and our lips intertwine. His tongue dips back into my mouth, and he lifts me slightly to shove himself back inside of me. I gasp as I slide back down, and his hands trace over my back, rubbing all over slowly as I start to ride him. He groans into me as I move faster, bouncing on his cock as my breasts fill the space between us. Our skin, wet and slippery together, and the only light source in the room is from the illuminated city buildings that pour into the space from the large windows we're up against. He moans loudly as he puts his hands under my thighs and drives into me relentlessly — faster and harder for what seems to be several minutes when suddenly his arms hug my waist tightly, keeping me still and locked in. I try to move, but he only shakes his head *no* as it falls to my chest. I rock my hips slightly, and his grip becomes tighter as he lifts his chin back up to look at me.

"I don't want to cum yet," his eyes full of sorrow and pain stricken as his breathing remains rapid. "I'm not ready for this to be over. I'm not ready...to lose you." He stammers softly as his head drops back down to my breasts.

I sigh loudly as the confusion wears on my eyes, and I grab each side of his face with both hands and tilt his chin up so we can look eye to eye. "I want to be with you." I say with the most matter-of-fact tone that I can. "Rhett, I love you. I can't imagine my life without you. You're not going to lose me." A soft smile appears on my face. I've never been more sure about anything in my life — he has to know this.

"But, what about..."

"We'll work through it, Rhett." I immediately cut him off.

His eyes seem lost, and his eyebrows burrow with force until a couple more seconds pass as I just stare at him...with the same gentle smile that's been stuck on my face. His features soften, and the ocean blue in his eyes brightens after it appears my words have finally sunken in. His jaw drops slightly, the corners of his lips curl upwards before his lips collide with mine, and his grip around my waist loosens. He lifts us off the couch and walks towards the bed — still, without pulling out of me. He lays me down gently, hunches over, and slowly thrusts into me from this angle. A muffled moan vibrates between our lips as I feel his cock, throbbing every time he pauses deep inside of me. My hands that were draped around his neck now rub down his chest — my fingers run along every bump and crevice of his abs, and he drives faster into me. My mouth releases from his as I cry out, and he straightens his posture, squeezing his hand around my throat as he pounds into me with force. I moan and feel that pent-up pressure in my core, needing to be released at this very moment. I relax fully, and a loud cry escapes as I feel the pressure free while I orgasm. The liquid pours out and splashes between us. Little specks trail up to his belly button and scatter on my legs.

"Fuck." Rhett drags out a loud groan as my wetness claps louder and louder as he thrusts. "Emilia...you're fucking mine."

I grin as I feel the pressure on my windpipe tighten, and raise my legs higher before I wrap them around his body and bring him closer to me. He leans down, moving his grip from the front of my neck to the back, as he plunges deep inside of me and kisses me with intent.

"Cum in my pussy Rhett." I sigh as our lips release. My gaze is fastened on his while his hand remains firm, my hair tangled between his fingers.

"You're fucking mine." He grins softly as our faces remain close.

"Cum, baby."

"Oh, you're fucking mine." His teeth grit as he squeezes tighter onto my neck.

I nod my head up and down, "Cum, baby."

"I'm gonna fucking cum."

I tighten my pussy around him, and he moans loudly as his thrusts become inconsistent. I feel his cock twitch inside of me as he falls on top of me, wrapping his arms around the top of my head to hold me. I tighten my arms around him in a hug and can't help but smile. He lifts up from me, pulling out of me before he lays down next to me on the perfectly made bed. His arm swings around my midriff as he pulls me in, nestling his face into my hair. He kisses the side of my head, and a giggle escapes from my lips. I can't help but feel anything but pure happiness. I turn my head to look at him, face to face, and his fingers lightly brush my cheek.

"I swear to God. I'm never letting you go, Emilia." He sighs once his breaths return to normal.

"Good." Is all I can muster before I feel the need to kiss his lips once more. "I'm starving," I whisper, smiling as my face remains close to his.

"Me too," he grins. "Chinese?"

"Oh my god, yes. I want —"

"Sesame Chicken, I know."

Chapter 26

Rhett

Watching Emilia eat Chinese has got to be one of my top five favorite things. She doesn't know how to use chopsticks — but she sure as hell tries.

"Do you want a fork?" I ask as my cheeks warm from my smile.

"No, I'm good." She says as she stabs a piece of chicken with one chopstick.

All I can do is shake my head slightly while my wide smile remains and for a moment I sit, and relish at how incredibly beautiful my life with her is going to be.

"Rhett?" She asks as her head pokes up from the white takeout box. "How come you made me get Plan B?"

I clear my throat, once again caught off guard at what comes out of her mouth. "Em, you're the first girl I've ever had sex with, without a condom…"

"Ha!" She snorts, "Yeah right."

"I'm serious, Emilia," I chuckle. "Cross my heart, swear — you're the first, and the last. But I didn't really make you." I say as my chin tilts down and my eyes follow suite.

"No?"

"Well, you kept saying I fucked you without a condom…I thought that was the appropriate response. I don't know Em, like I said — I've never done that before. But it couldn't have been a bad idea, because you're only twenty-one…if we want a miracle to happen, don't you want me to put a ring on your finger first?"

"Rhett…" she says softly.

"Yes?" I question, only, more prepared for it.

"How come you cant…"

I don't even let her finish before I start in, "Remember when I got into that huge fight?"

"With the three guys in California?"

"Yes, well, three against one was hard to beat —"

"But we took you to the hospital…I was there, I mean…I never knew…"

"Well, it wasn't until a couple of months after — you guys were already in Texas, and I kept having the same pain, the same symptoms, My mom took me to get checked and I think with the trauma and scar tissue that built up...it just was over from there. My mom made me do all these tests, I mean, just ridiculous things for a teenager, but all these tests came with the same results."

"Rhett..." she stops me, "It's my fault." Her eyes fall heavy while they gloss over, becoming small pools of water.

"It's not." I assure her.

"It is. You fought them...because of me."

"Em, it was my choice to get into it with three dudes twice my size, without any backup. I did it to myself, I promise you. He was harassing you the night before. *I* saw him out the next day, *I* confronted him, *I* chose to do what I did. Not you."

Her hand cups her mouth as her eyes squeeze shut and tears stream down her cheeks. I set my takeout box of rice on the bed and walk over to her. My arms wrap around her waist as I kneel to the ground and hold her. My head rests on her chest while she sits in the desk chair, her arms wrap around my body and squeeze as her sobs become more prominent. This isn't her fault, and if I have to spend the rest of my life making it known to her, I will.

"Emilia, please," I say as my head lifts up and I cup her rosy cheeks with my hands.

"I'm sorry," She whispers. Her voice strained and cracked.

I kiss her lips softly and her crying subsides. Seeing Emilia upset is one of my least favorite sites, so if I have to kiss her every time to fix it, so help me God, I will.

After some moments of silence, a few more kisses, and one big hug, we continue eating — laughing and talking through it all until we're tired enough to crawl into bed. I know we need to sleep, but she makes it hard to want to close my eyes. Closing my eyes means I have to stop looking at her, and if I were to live a thousand lives, I would hate that idea in every single one. My fingers twirl small strands of her hair that frame her face. I touch her as gently as possible, only to make sure she can fall asleep. The color of each strand varies, some are deeper browns mixed with milk chocolate and I brush my thumb over the different colors.

"What about adoption?" She murmurs softly.

"Always a possibility," I match her tone.

"We have a while to go until then, but there's a lot of precious babies that need our love." She smiles gently with her eyes closed.

All I can do is grin, in the sheer fact that a future with her is even an option. My hand moves to her face, tracing lightly over her cheek as her eyes try to stay open, I give her a soft smile, and she gives one in return. My thumb grazes on top of her eyebrow, lightly gliding along her skin to put her to sleep.

"Dog walks, taxes, coffee..." she mumbles softly as her eyes flutter shut. "I want all of it, with you."

Chapter 27
Emilia

When I woke up this morning, the only thought running through my head was how sure I was with my decision. My life has never been normal. It's been full of changes, inconsistency, and temporariness. Rhett is one of the two people who has remained constant in it, never faltering or wavering.

The things I thought I wanted most seem insignificant compared to how my soul feels when I'm with him. The funny thing about life is — you think you have it planned out to a T — *I want to be married when I'm twenty-six, I want to start having children when I'm twenty-eight*, shit like that causes stress and...deadlines. Why would anyone put deadlines and time limits on their life, as if careers don't do enough of it. Childish, it's childish to think that fate, destiny, or some fucked up grand scheme isn't waiting around the corner, getting ready to mess up your plans. Roll with life, be happy, and be *free* — no sense in trying to plan a future when the future is not meant to be planned.

As we get into Rhett's blacked-out truck, his hand reaches over his center counsel to grab just above my knee. I grin as I turn my head to look at him. "You're going to talk to Ford today?" I ask.

"I am."

"And then pick me up after work?"

"I am." He nods.

I smile as I grab his hand and stare ahead, red light after red light, until we pull in front of my apartment complex.

"Emilia, after your lease is up...would you...want to move in...with me?" He stutters softly once the car is parked.

"Why wait?"

"Well, it's not as nice as yours. I just figured you might want to stay there as long as possible."

"I don't give a shit how nice it is. I'd rather be with you in a shack than without you at all." My eyes flutter to his hands that wipe on his pants as if he's nervous. "What if we found another place together and split the rent?"

"You're not fucking paying for anything, Emilia." He scoffs with a smile.

"Then your dirty slums it is." I giggle.

"It's not a dirty —"

"I'm just kidding. I'm sure it's a nice place." I smile close to his face before I kiss him again and open the door. "After work, right?"

"After work." He assures me with a smile, and I shut the passenger door and make my way to the front entrance.

I turn back to the street before I walk in, only to see Rhett's car — still parked.

"You can leave, Rhett," I shout to him.

"I'm waiting until you get inside." He yells from the open passenger window.

My eyes roll to the back of my head as I let out a deep laugh and push through the doors to walk in.

I would think at least a small part of me feels mournful at the thought of the future I wanted. But the reality is that family to me isn't having a house full of kids running around anymore.

Family is *him*.

All the years, me thinking I never had a place to call home…home is whenever I'm with *him*.

Love isn't rational. Sometimes it doesn't make sense. It can make you do stupid things, and you find it in the most arbitrary places — *but when you feel it* — when you really feel it, it just makes sense.

I was the exception.

And he is mine.

Acknowledgments

A huge thank you to my friends and family for the continued support as I keep writing. To my new friends, who have loved my first book — I hope you love this one just as much. The amount of love and appreciation I have seen since the release of my debut novel has been unmatched and I just want to say thank you, again, from the bottom of my heart. To my mom, Arlene — you promised you would read this and not speak a word of it to me, you've done a pretty good job, and for that...I thank you. I'm glad you enjoyed it, but I don't need to know exactly why. You are the light of my life, and I'm happy I've gotten you to read TWO books in the span of a year, a huge accomplishment on my part. To my sister, Dani — your support, on everything I have done...ever...does not go unnoticed. I hope everyone in the world has a big sister as thoughtful, caring, smart, and beautiful as you. To Brooke — I roped you into my journey of writing, and I can't thank you enough for continually helping and critiquing me along the way. I know I wrote a decent book when you like it, so it gives me the confidence boost I so desperately need to publish. I appreciate our friendship, our morning breakfast dates with our specialty coffees, and everything else we do together. To everyone who has reached out about their love for my first novel...it's overwhelming (the good kind), to know what you think — and how much you loved it. I appreciate each and every one of you who said "I can't wait until the next one." Well, it's here, and it got a little rough in there...pun intended. But I hope it did not disappoint. To my new, little ARC team that has been formed — thank you for wanting to be a part of my crazy journey, I hope you stick with me for the long haul. To my editor and cover designer — I can't say enough good things. Thank you, for your creativity, your knowledge, and above all, for being absolute rockstars. And of course, My husband and my children. I love you all dearly, I'm still so sorry you are not allowed to read this yet, Payton...but to be honest, I don't think I'll ever let you read this one. To Vinny, my sweet boy...thank you for telling all of the kids in your class that your mommy is an author, it makes me feel really cool. I love you all...and appreciate every one of you. On to the next!

About Author

Madeline Flagel is a mom with two kids who are in every sport imaginable. So while free time is sparse, she does enjoy reading and travel. She's a beach bum, Chicago Cubs fan, and an entrepreneur, starting and selling many companies throughout her career. Madeline is an avid reader of romance novels and an even spicier writer of the genre.

Also By

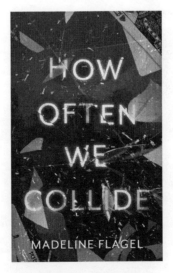

NOW on Amazon

Made in the USA
Monee, IL
19 June 2023